Discovering David

Cherri Kimball Neal-Kneel

Forward

Many years ago, when David was young, God spoke to his aunt telling her a book was to be written for him. Through the years, she and I talked about her writing it. She often said, “I’d better get that book written,” or I would say it to her. When he was 6, a strange thing happened. I woke up one morning to discover some strange papers lying on my kitchen counter. I had cleaned them the night before, so I was surprised to see a pile of papers. They were in my sister’s handwriting. I looked through my house expecting to find her. I thought she must have snuck in through the night to surprise me. She was nowhere to be found in my northern CA home. I called her in Idaho and told her what I had found. She was surprised and asked me what they said. I read a few words. She responded with even more surprise. “Those are my notes for David’s book! How did they get there?” I told her I didn’t know.

I laughed and said, “God must have hand-delivered them.” I told her, “God must be serious about wanting you to write it!” We were both amazed.

For the next few years, we laughed and talked about that experience and about how she needed to get David’s book written. It never happened. To the day of her death, we discussed it, but she never wrote it. I have long lost those papers. I never read them past the few words I read her on that day. I do not know what they said. I do not remember the few words I read her.

One day, after my sister was gone, I was telling someone the story about God hand-delivering the papers. It came to me for the first time that he brought them to me! He wanted me to write David's story all along. It was good that I didn't know that. It was His timing. I know now what the notes may have said only because He gave me the book from David's life itself. The experiences in this book came from knowing David.

I had a dream about David long before he was conceived. I was told his name; and, I was shown his face. In the dream, he was 24. This book just happened to be written the early months of his 24th year of life. None of this was planned to occur this way. It happened this way because it was planned by God Himself, as were the experiences David has lived through for this story to be written. It had to come after David himself had decided he needed to take a walkabout to discover God. I hope you enjoy the journey God takes him on in this book.

Acknowledgements

I would like to extend a personal thank you to the many people who helped bring this book into being.

Bethany Erline Foraker (Petey), thank you for being my sister, my friend, my prayer partner, my advocate, and my mother when a mom wasn't available. Thank you for inspiring me to write, encouraging me with a lifetime of applause, and being there for me to the very end. I am glad you are already there in that beautiful place where David begins this journey. This is for you!

Thank you, Chris, my precious husband who always puts his money where his mouth is to ensure my success. You are my biggest fan and I am yours!

Many thanks go to all my children and grandchildren, the ones here and the ones waiting for me there, who always make me want to try harder.

Thank you to Earl Kimball, the man who my real Papa put in charge of me while I am here on this earth. Thanks for teaching me that I could be and do anything if I tried hard enough!

Thank you to my sister, Rebecca, who taught me to "make it happen."

Mostly, a huge thank you goes to David who helped me put this experience into words by sharing the things in detail I didn't know how to write. If it were not for him, this book would not have been written.

Discovering David

Chapter 1

David stepped into the cold, unlit room. The smell of mildew and mold hit his nostrils tantalizing an allergic response to flare up instantly. He lifted his forearm in an unconscious effort to protect his nose and mouth. Using his free arm, he felt around in the dark room. His eyes were beginning to adjust and he could just make out a shadowy outline of an old desk. He could feel his lungs tightening from trying not to breathe too much of the damp and musky air inside the room. As he stepped closer to the desk, he reached out and felt the layers of damp papers stacked on the top. He had been in this room the night before. He knew that he had reached the goal of tonight's dark and stealthy adventure.

Last night, David had been walking down the tree-ridden lane that veered off the highway he had been hiking on. He had left his home on the Central Coast of California on what his mom called a walkabout. Something deep inside had created an urge for adventure and discovery he couldn't shake. He wasn't sure what he wanted to discover or even what was drawing him. He had mulled it over on many sleepless nights. He was sure he wanted something more. He was sure that what he was doing could not be all there was meant to be for his life. He felt called to something deeper. Was he being called into some adventure; or, was he being deceived and led into some sinister plot that would end his purpose, or at least steer him in the wrong direction? He wasn't sure.

At 24, he felt invincible. The urge was stronger and more interesting than the daily grind as a manager of a hot rod store where he sat behind a desk, bored most of the time. He had spent many nights praying to God, wanting this life he was stuck in to mean something. Sometimes, he just wanted to find God. He hoped that finding God would help him feel there was a purpose to something.

Other times, he prayed to find a person to fill his emptiness. He had felt lonely most of his life even when others were around. He had trouble sleeping. He sought answers during the darkness of night, his mind racing with nagging thoughts and questions. He felt deeply alone. He was troubled. Most people who knew him would not have seen him that way. He was kind. He was witty. He was intelligent and fairly self-educated from reading and studying interesting ideas and concepts. By nature, he was a philosopher of sorts.

He loved to have long conversations where he could share his deep thoughts and listen to others' thoughts about things like life, the universe, reasons, and what-ifs. He dreamed of inventing machines and unusual operational problem-solvers he was sure no one had thought of. He imagined developing new kinds of artificial limbs, energy-free engines, and time-warp traveling mechanisms.

He dreamed of exploring the depths of the human mind and its untapped capabilities.

He carried on conversations with those who would listen. He talked at length about dimensions that existed beyond the one we were stuck in. He imagined and created ways to explore them. His soul was not settled. His soul was restless.

There was also the desire for a companion. He desperately wanted to have a relationship with someone who could match his soul. He didn't want any more surface friendships. He certainly did not need any more game-playing girlfriends. He had never been very good at playing games. It was too much work. He had to have something true, something real. No one seemed to fit that bill.

He had experienced having a broken heart more than once. He had broken a few hearts himself. He was tired of it all and wanted something real, someone real. He wanted to feel like he belonged to someone, like he mattered to someone, and that he was understood by someone. He wanted to talk and be heard, really heard. He wanted to feel respected and desired. Something had to be real and he was very tired of waiting.

He had searched for a while, given up for a while, and searched again. He had spent the last few months really trying to put it all aside and seek God, hoping that would somehow heal that empty desperate need for more than just existing day by day. He was tired of life. He was tired of going to work, eating food, trying to sleep, and tired of the relentless thoughts that kept him awake. He was tired of being tired. He was lonely for answers. He was lonely for friendship. He was lonely for love and acceptance. He wanted to belong, to matter, to have a purpose and a reason.

His mother had told him over and over he would find those things in God only. She had said many times he would find God only when he searched for God with all his heart. He didn't know how to search with all his heart. He tried. Things always got in the way. Life got in the way. How can your whole heart search if you have to live life? One still has to eat. One still has to work. One still wants to love and be loved. One still has to talk and move around. Distractions exist everywhere.

Late one night, he had packed a small backpack with a change of clothes, a few pair of socks, and a rain jacket. Tying a rolled up sleeping bag to the bottom of the backpack, he had headed out in search of that something he longed for. With two weeks' pay in his pocket and his hunger for something bigger than himself and his mundane existence, he left his family and the comforts of home. Maybe he could search for God if he left all distractions behind. Maybe he would at least find answers. Maybe… who knew? Anything had to be better than just waking up tomorrow and doing the same thing until darkness hit; at which time, he'd be left alone again to think and wish till day broke in on his lonely soul and tired body.

After traveling for as long as he could on foot, he had taken this lane last night, lured by the leaves dancing in the breeze and the conversations of birds hiding in the branches and grasses growing around a barbed-wire fence. The fence had at one time isolated a field on one side from the gravel of the lane. It was now broken down with time, aged by weather and wind. The night before, he had walked along listening to nature, enjoying the breeze and shelter of shade. He had planned to hunt his own food and live off the land, forgetting this was the 21st Century. Wildlife was not readily available and when it was, it was something to look at or listen to. It didn't even resemble food. Hunger pangs and sore feet forced him to sit and rest.

He had only been on his walkabout for about 6 hours and already adventure wasn't as inviting as it had been when he began the journey. He had looked around hoping to see something he could eat. There were no boxes or cans and there was definitely a scarcity of fast food places. He had pulled the backpack off his aching shoulders and wiped his sweaty face as he sat down on the side of the road with his throbbing head balanced on a deteriorating, wobbly fence post.

Closing his eyes, he had dreamed about the wonders of a boring job, tacos, soda, and his mother's hug in the morning at Starbucks. He had been so desperate to escape all of those things. Now, it all seemed as appealing as getting away had been before. Even in his dreams, he wondered at his own discontentment. He wondered if he would ever find that rest of soul he was seeking.

It was dusk when he had awakened. He had realized it would soon be dark and he would be alone on this strange road to nowhere. Once again, he had wiped his tired eyes, feeling a sharp pain in his stomach. He had dropped his hands and pushed himself up. He'd stood up on tired and achy legs, noticing a shed out in the field across the lane. He had not seen it in the daylight. Shadows and shapes had developed in the darkness. Sounds that didn't sound familiar or safe had begun to erupt from the grass and trees. Swallowing away the sense of fear that was stirring up inside, he had pulled up the heavy backpack and hurried to the shed, noticing his heart was racing more than it should for such a brave adventurer.

Kicking open the door, he had almost fallen inside quickly shutting the door behind him. It had grown dark, but he was able to see an army cot on the far wall and a desk covered with papers and pencils in the center where the window must give its light in the mornings.

He had curiously walked to the desk trying to get a closer look at the papers. He had hoped to find an empty one, so he could sketch a little in the dimming light, hoping to also dim his loneliness and fear. He had found one piece of paper that appeared to be clean and a pencil sharpened and ready for use. Sitting on the army cot with his back against the wall, he had tried to sketch a motor of the car he wished to design. The night fell quickly. He had drawn without clear vision until he could see no longer. He had finally fallen into a deep sleep.

When he awoke in the morning, he had found himself back under a tree on the dry dusty lane with birds singing a wakeup call. Once again, his heart had begun to race! How had he ended up on the road again? "Was I dreaming?" He had felt comforted by the sound of his own voice. He had felt his arm and face to see if he was dreaming or awake. He had looked across the lane to see if he could see the shed. The field was empty except for the dry grass waving at him. He had spoken aloud again, hoping to feel the same comfort. "Maybe I am too hungry to think straight."

David had spent the entirety of the day in the shade of the trees listening to birds and watching dancing grass. He had been determined to see if that shed showed up again or if he had been dreaming. A few times throughout the day, he had acknowledged that he was being ridiculous. No shed was in the field. He was hot, tired, and hungry. His mind was playing tricks on him. He must have fallen asleep on the dusty lane and dreamed about the shed. Still, he couldn't shake the feeling that it had really been there. He had to know, despite desperately needing to find something to eat. When dusk came, he had awakened from an afternoon doze and once again had seen the outline of the shed.

Now, here he was, ready to find out what he could discover about last night's experience. He must not have been dreaming. He tried not to think about the absence of the shed in the daylight. He walked inside.

The papers on the desk were damp and the smell was even stronger tonight. "How are they getting so damp?" He asked out loud. Since David's original reason for wanting a walkabout experience had been to see if he could find a way to discover God, and since his own voice was so comforting, he decided it would be best to converse with God out loud. He really wasn't expecting an audible answer although he hoped he might get one. Maybe He would actually talk back. Instead, the odor of mold grew stronger causing him to sneeze several times in a row.

There was just enough light to notice his drawing on the cot. He stumbled over some books and sat on the cot wiping his nose on an old napkin in his pocket. He wondered if he should spend another night in this place. As he walked to the door, paper and pencil in hand, he heard a strange noise and stopped. Again, his heart was racing as he tried to muster up his adventurous spirit. After a few seconds, he realized he was forgetting to breathe. He drew in a deep breath which caused him to begin sneezing again.

Trying to forget the unusual noise, he moved closer to the door and reached for the handle only to be startled by another strange noise. He wiped his nose again and returned to the cot to draw until the light faded. He dozed off sitting on the cot.

Sometime in the night, he awakened expecting to be on the road again. He realized it was still night and he was still in the shed. He could smell something he hadn't noticed before. He slowly stood up and felt his way to the smell. It smelled like a mixture of roses, candles, and bread. The smell was very faint, but definitely there, mingled in with the smell of mold. He reached around in the dark trying to find what it was. His hand touched something hard and cold. Feeling it carefully from top to bottom, he realized it was a goblet of some sort. He lifted it and smelled the contents wondering what it was that could smell like that in a place like this. He couldn't see the contents. He tried to make his eyes adjust, lifting the goblet for another smell.

Carefully, he placed his lips against the rim and tipped it slightly to taste the contents. It tasted like water. He took a little sip to be sure. Yes, it was water. "Maybe the smell is from something else," he thought. He was so thirsty and hungry! He kept taking careful sips until the goblet was empty. He sat it back down, noticing the smell had vanished. He sneezed again.

David walked carefully back to the cot feeling somewhat refreshed. This time, he lied down and faced straight up hoping to avoid dust and mold on the cot. Falling into a deep sleep, he dreamed of car engines and birds singing.

David startled awake! He realized he was actually hearing an engine and birds. He sat up, his back aching from lying on the hard and dusty lane. He brushed off pebbles that had indented themselves into his elbows. The engine of a small tractor passing by caused some of the birds to rush to higher branches and whisper to each other. He held his sleeve over his nose as the tractor passed. "That's all I need, more dust," he thought.

The tractor stopped a few feet past him. A man dressed in a plaid shirt and bib overalls jumped down holding onto a straw hat atop his dark, curly locks. He smiled. His white-toothed grin contrasted sharply with his dark, tanned skin. He was chewing on a piece of straw. The man walked casually over to David and reached out a gloved hand to him. David took his hand and helped himself up realizing this gesture was probably for a handshake not to help him to his feet. He felt his face flush a little in the realization. The farmer smiled with a twinkle in his amber-colored eyes.

"Look a little sore, Friend," the farmer's look seemed to be poking fun at him, but in such a friendly way, David wasn't offended at all.

"Yeah, just a little," David smiled in response.

"Hungry?" asked the farmer.

"Yeah, just a little." David realized he had repeated himself. The farmer sauntered over to the tractor, reached into a basket, and pulled out a sandwich and a thermos of lemonade. Sitting down where David had been sitting, he opened up the sandwich and handed David half of it along with the thermos. David gingerly took the sandwich and thermos thinking of how he couldn't drink after someone else, but really wanting to have a drink.

The man's eyes twinkled again, "Go ahead, have a drink. I haven't touched it yet." He took a huge bite out of his half of the sandwich mid-sentence. David wondered if he had known what he was thinking or was just making conversation. He opened the thermos and drank several gulps of cold lemonade. He ate his half of the sandwich trying not to look as hungry as he really was. The tuna and mayonnaise were mixed to perfection, just the way David liked his tuna made. The crispy pickles, lettuce, and tomatoes made the sandwich a meal. David savored every bite.

The farmer still had not reached for the thermos, so David wiped his mouth and took a few more gulps. "Wow! Thanks," David was truly thankful for his first meal living off the land. He hadn't expected it to come that way. The farmer took a few drinks from the thermos and walked back to his tractor. He jumped up on the seat, started the engine, and turned to smile at David, tossing him a bag as he started off down the lane. "Wait!" David yelled, realizing he should have asked about the shed. The engine was too loud.

David scrambled to get to his feet, but his legs were too weak and sore too move fast; and, he didn't feel like jogging to catch up. "Besides," He thought out loud, "How can I ask him about a shed I don't even see right now. He will think I am crazy. Maybe I am. Maybe this food will clear my head."

He started to pick up his pack and move on, but looking at the field, he decided he would stay till evening and see if the shed appeared when he wasn't so tired and hungry. He just had to know. He lied down in the shade of the tree and slept most of the afternoon enjoying his full stomach. He forgot to look in the bag the farmer had tossed him. When he woke up, it was past dusk. It was truly dark. A full moon illuminated the field and the stars twinkled above the shed, which was now very visible again.

David was sure his head was clear and that he was awake. That realization really didn't help in the dark though. It made the shed's appearance a little more fearful this time. He really couldn't see this shed in the daylight. He could see it clearly in the dark. It was damp and moldy; yet, it sat in a field of grass dried by midday heat. David wondered if he should go inside it again. He sat down and stared at the shed for about an hour wondering what he should do. The moon was full. He picked up the bag the farmer had left and opened it up, peering into it with the light of the moon and stars. He could smell something that seemed strangely similar to the smell in the shed the night before. It faintly smelled like roses, candles, and bread.

He reached his hand inside and found seven small biscuits. When he tasted them, they tasted differently than they smelled. They reminded him of his mother's whole wheat biscuits with honey and butter. He ate three of them, closing the sack to save the rest. It seemed a great sacrifice to wait for them, but he knew he would be hungry in the morning.

David walked to the shed. He could see very clearly tonight. He pushed the door open and the moldy smell rushed his nostrils. He walked inside, leaving the door open for air and light from the moon. He walked to the desk and moved some of the papers around wishing he could make out what was on them.

The goblet was still on the table by the cot. He made his way across the room much easier tonight stepping over boxes and books. He picked up the goblet. There was no smell tonight, but it was full of water again. He tasted it, spitting it out immediately. The taste of the water was as moldy as the room itself. He wondered if he had drunk something bad the night before not realizing it because of his thirst. Maybe the mold had affected his mind or his eyes. He sat down on the cot and pulled out another biscuit to remove the moldy taste from his mouth. One after the other, he compromised his morning meal and finished off the biscuits while he continued his sketch on the paper.

David awakened with a dry mouth and sand-filled eyes lying beside the lane. The tractor was just down the lane. It must have come by earlier stirring up dust. He rubbed his eyes and blinked wildly trying to get the sand out. He looked around hoping to see the farmer, or at least his thermos. Neither was anywhere to be seen. The shed was missing from across the road.

David stood up slowly, aware that his pants were very loose from wear and probably from the loss of several pounds over the last few days.

"I'm not getting very far on this journey," he spoke out loud. David looked at the empty field, shook his head in a gesture of sarcastic self-disgust, and picked up his backpack to begin his journey. As he bent over to pick up the empty sack from the farmer's biscuits, a pencil fell out of his shirt pocket. David drew in a sharp breath! He felt adrenaline rush through his body. It was the pencil from the shed, freshly sharpened and half-used. He felt stuck, paralyzed, as he bent over the pencil lying on the ground. He tried to think. He didn't bring that pencil and forget about it in his hunger did he?

No, he was sure it was from the shed. He had forgotten to bring anything to draw with and had planned to find a store where he could purchase a tablet and pencil to carry with him. He stayed bent over that pencil, breathing in loud breaths, and feeling the adrenaline pump through him. This was the pencil from the shed! There was a shed! Still bending over, he looked out into the field. Why couldn't he see it in the daylight? If it wasn't real, how did this pencil get in his pocket? He was confused. He picked up the pencil and slowly stood, turning toward the field and staring incessantly at it.

Leaving his backpack, he crossed the lane and walked out into the field looking for evidence of the shed. Something strange was happening. Fear was subsiding. David felt a surge of strength and determination. He was not going to leave. He was going to find out what was happening. His mind was racing.

"This is so cool!" This time he didn't speak out loud for comfort. He was voicing his excitement of adventure. "This is so cool!" he repeated with a smile and a giggle. His legs felt stronger. His head was not throbbing. He held up the pencil and smiled right at it with determination. "This is so cool" he repeated a third time, anxious for night to fall this time.

David didn't fall asleep for his usual afternoon nap here by the gravel lane. He kept watching the field with a smile and a little head nod every now and then, a challenge in his eyes and in his heart. The tractor was still parked on the road. David wondered where the farmer was and why he had deserted the tractor for so long. He hoped he would see him. A sandwich would be nice.

"The lemonade would be even better," he thought as he swallowed, trying to clear away the dryness in his mouth. Afternoon shadows were falling when he noticed a bag on the side of the tractor. It was a bag just like the one with biscuits the day before. David walked over, looking around for the farmer. He couldn't see the farmer anywhere. His hunger was so strong that he peeked into the bag just to get a smell. The faint scent of roses, candles, and bread crossed his nostrils and he heard a step in the pebbles on the lane.

"Thought you might need a snack," the farmer said stepping up behind David, who immediately flushed from embarrassment. It was not indicative of his character to snoop in someone else's belongings. He was not a thief. Yet, here he was peering into the farmer's bag on the farmer's tractor.

"Go ahead. It's for you," the farmer motioned with his gloved hand. David was so embarrassed, he just stood there. "Go ahead." The farmer motioned again, with a smile and a twinkle of amusement in his amber eyes.

David muttered, "Thanks," then tried to explain. "Sorry, I just wanted to get a smell. I wasn't going to take it." The farmer kept smiling and looking at him. David felt like his excuse was pretty lame for his bad behavior.

"It's for you. Take it," the farmer said, swinging a sickle onto the back of the tractor. He handed David the bag and the thermos. "See you later." The tractor started off with a jerk. David remembered to ask him about the shed this time, but couldn't bring himself to say a word. He held the bag and thermos, staring at the farmer and the tractor as it chugged its way on down the lane. When he turned around to the spot by the fence where he had been resting, he saw a basket with three white napkins lying across the top. He looked back at the tractor, but it wasn't there. It must have driven around a bend or driven off into a field. The farmer must have left the basket there before he walked up behind David.

Suddenly, David wasn't embarrassed anymore. Somehow it all fit together. Once again, he spoke out loud. "This is so cool." He looked up, speaking to God. "Wow, either I am really losing it or this is way cool." He opened the bag first and discovered seven little biscuits. He took one out to eat while he opened the thermos for a long, cold drink of lemonade. He reached to open the basket with a smile so big his cheeks were actually hurting. Inside the basket, he discovered two large sandwiches made with thick homemade bread, two apples, some green grapes, a large bottle of water, and three large homemade chocolate chip cookies. He ate one of the sandwiches, drank the lemonade, and finished with an apple and a cookie. Placing the bag of biscuits in the basket, he sat back awaiting dusk.

David didn't waste the time as he sat waiting. He was developing a plan as he watched for the shed to appear. When dusk fell, he was still watching the field. Yet, no shed appeared. He was beginning to doubt again as he fumbled with the pencil. He leaned over to get the bottle of water out of the basket. When he looked up, he could see the outline of the shed in the field. The first part of his plan had failed. He had missed seeing it appear. Still, he had a strategy.

Picking up his backpack and the basket, he wondered across the field looking at all the landmarks he could see, each tree etched in his mind. A fallen tree stump with tangled berries around it rested about three feet to the left of the shed. He walked around the shed. Just behind it, there was a small clump of wild roses. He wondered if this was where the scent had come from previously. Maybe the wind had carried the scent across the lane as he had opened the first biscuit bag as well. He leaned over to smell the roses for familiarity. A thorn scratched his hand as he reached to pick one. He jerked his hand away, deciding he would pick one tomorrow in the light, and then he continued around the shed to the right side where three large stones were piled in a heap beside a small bunch of weeds.

David walked into the shed leaving the door open again for air. He found his sketch and turned it over scribbling the locations of the landmarks on the back. Turning it over again, he sat back to sketch until it was too dark to see. When he felt himself getting drowsy, he stood up and felt around the shed. He would not fall asleep this night!

The night dragged on. Time seemed to be standing still. He sipped his water so he would have some for the long, hot day tomorrow. He ate a biscuit, got up, and wondered around the shed. He sat back down and sipped again, and then ate another two biscuits. He walked over and felt around the desk. It was still dark. He picked up a few pages of paper off the desk, walked over to the cot, and folded them up along with his sketch. He placed the papers inside his shirt and put the pencil in his pocket, feeling them every few minutes to be sure they were still in place. He was determined not to sleep. The night seemed to last for days and his food had dwindled down to one lone biscuit and a sip of water. He was desperately trying to stay awake as hour after hour passed, and he was sure, day after day until he could no longer care. He drifted off with a heavy sigh, resting his head on the papers on the desk.

He awoke with a start as he realized he was sitting on the hard gravel with his head hanging into the empty basket on his lap.

"Must have been hungry." It was the farmer's voice. David felt a little dizzy and foggy as he looked up. He felt like he had been awake for days and had just drifted off for a minute. His eyes felt sore and tired. He reached to feel in his shirt pocket, too tired to mutter a response to the farmer. He leaned back with a long, uncontrolled sigh as he pulled out the folded papers and felt for the pencil still lingering in his pocket. A faint smile crossed his lips as he drifted off again.

Startling awake, he realized the farmer was gone. Wildly, he felt for the papers. They were still there, lying on his lap. The pencil was still sitting in his pocket. Beside him, there was a full thermos and a basket full of bread, cheese, fruit wine, and a can of sardines. All of which he devoured to the last drop before opening the pages that were lying beside him now on the pebbles, next to another bag of biscuits and a bottle of water. He looked at the field hoping to see the shed. It was not there and neither were any of the landmarks he had jotted down. There was only the open field with dry grasses beckoning in the breeze with a friendly wave.

David looked at the pages he had taken off the desk. Each had sketches of a strange design. All together, they made one picture of a vehicle. It was elongated, pointed on both ends. Strange equations were jotted all around the pages. Half sentences describing engine parts and movements were scribbled along the sides of one page. He studied them for a few minutes trying to make sense of them.

A creeping realization came over him, starting in his toes and radiating through his head, and then outward to his fingertips as the adrenaline pumped through his entire body once again.

"No way," he whispered to himself in utter amazement. Slowly, he opened the sketch he had been working on comparing it to the half sentences and descriptions jotted on the page he was holding from the desk in the shed. David calculated the dimensions of the engine hull of the strange vehicle sketched on the pages with the calculations he had imagined as he sketched the engine he was designing. He had really been playing around. It wasn't one of the engines or designs he usually drew.

This one had been unrealistic, too powerful to use in any real vehicle. He had designed it with thoughts of quantum physics, light years, and travel through other dimensions of reality. It was play really, something he and his mother used to discuss together, play theories in their what-if games. He had been playing around in order to get lost in his design and not feel the darkness creeping in, or the fear or loneliness that came calling those nights in the shed. "No way! This is way cool!" He whispered, aware that his vocabulary had become slightly limited lately.

David studied the design of the motor, turning it to the right and then to the left. He turned it completely upside down and then right-side up again. He nodded to himself. "It would work! Oh yeah, it would work!" He felt so energized he wanted to do something. He was so excited. He didn't feel like sitting still. Yet, he couldn't, or wouldn't, stop staring at the motor. He was enjoying what he could see and what he could imagine in the possibilities of what he had drawn and in what he was discovering in the papers from the shed, the shed that appeared and disappeared, the shed that didn't seem real in the daylight hours except for what he had taken from it at night into the daylight.

He had begun this walkabout to get closer to God. He leaned his head back against the post to think. Maybe he was going to have an experience with God. This whole shed thing was strange and surreal. Maybe it wasn't even really happening. Maybe he was having a vision. Maybe he was dreaming the whole thing. After all, dreams can be very confusing and seem so real. Why couldn't God just show up? After all, he was making a huge effort to spend time alone with Him. Here he was, out on the road away from any comforts of home, with no food, and giving up everything he had personally acquired just to be with Him. He had been willing to live off the land and sacrifice everything just to be with Him. "Yes, it is cool that I have been given food by that guy," he pondered. "But, it doesn't seem quite the same as finding food provided by God."

The sound in the pebbles startled David out of his thoughts. "How's it going, Friend?" It was the farmer. David reached out to shake the offered hand this time. The glove felt soft and worn with stiffened creases.

"Going okay," answered David as he unconsciously looked for a basket or sack.

“Going to be warm today,” the farmer said, wiping the back of his glove along His forehead. “Yup, going to be warm.” He looked at David straight in the eyes. David answered with a nod, getting up on his own this time. He wiped off his jeans realizing the futility of the gesture since they had not been washed for days and were sagging and wrinkled into dirt filled crevices now. He looked up slightly embarrassed.

The farmer smiled knowingly and David dropped his eyes, not sure how to respond to the farmer’s expression. It had no judgment, only a kind understanding look that made David feel uncomfortable and comfortable at the same time.

“I like to hit the swimming hole this time of the year.” The farmer was sauntering off. “It’s just around the bend there,” he said, pointing the way. David quickly gathered up his belongings. He carefully folded the pages and grabbed his backpack up in one swing to catch up to the farmer.

“I’ve been drawing something.” David felt stupid the minute he said it. He wasn’t sure why he had blurted out something like that to a complete stranger. The farmer looked up. He was silent, but looked at David to finish what he was saying. David wasn’t sure what to say now. He was feeling very child-like and was wanting not to at the same time. He stood up straighter into his full 6’ 2” and continued, not knowing for sure what else to do at this point. "I was drawing a motor, trying to pass the time."

"Before what?" the farmer asked.

David stared blankly, and then he answered with a smile. "Good question." The farmer smiled back and they walked on in silence to the bend in the road.

He was thinking now about the design of the motor as he walked along. "How much energy is produced by the momentum of the earth?" he thought. The design he had drawn was racing through his mind. There was a problem with the motor he had designed and he needed to solve it. His mind began to race with thoughts of engines and time travel.

"It would provide such a continual source of energy, travel at any speed may be possible; but, the source could not be turned off and would continue output. The problem is that it has a molten core like the earth. Stopping it would cause the core to harden and would destroy the source of energy. The materials needed would be hard to come by. I would need alloys unaffected by heat up to 3 to 4 thousand degrees," he thought.

He continued to invent his engine in his mind as he walked, lost in his own fractured thoughts of designs and possibilities. "I'd need hundreds of magnets of different sizes and strengths, alloy rods, and springs. Also, tools that could provide perfect cuts and bends, tools to drill and perfect orbs made of alloys that could provide both the motor and casing. How could I make momentum and build around sphere by sphere? To extract the energy is even harder. Having to have the contacts and having to be so precise as well as the inward feeding of the motor would be more than difficult. The strength of the casing would have to be well thought out, all without taking away from the contacts or limiting space and loosing needed energy. To accelerate would not be hard; but, to cool it at accelerated rates would be."

He continued on, lost in the imaginations of exciting and unrealistic possibilities, "At the same time, the cooler it is the faster and more efficient the motor would be. Still, I am unsure of the magnitude of force it could create or how I can make that work to create more energy as well as keeping it contained. The x factor is what worries me. The expansion of the core could be catastrophic and would do more than just destroy the motor. It would kill me and maybe more. How hot would it get? What would the expansion of the rest of the materials be? What would need to expand, and what would need to stay? Also, the casing would be in danger. It would need to expand at the same rate, but not get off course with the rest of the motor or the magnetic swinging arms. Too much possibility! Too much danger! No way of finding out the energy created even if the materials were to be found."

David's mind continued to entertain him as he trudged along, unaware of anything around him. He smiled briefly as he realized if anyone had been able to hear his thoughts, they might have thought that he was rambling like a mad-man. No one had ever really understood him. Even those who pretended to listen were unable to follow his thoughts. He continued to think as he walked.

"However, the idea of the energy that would have to be expelled could make way for safe travel. Using liquid plasma in an electrically charged manner and in multiple layers, distance and shielding would never be an issue, as well as being a way of allowing needed energy a place to go. This, of course would only be needed for travel at rates yet unexplored." His mind was racing through magnets, turning objects, and thoughts of time and speed.

The farmer was just surfacing from his dive into the turquoise water hole fed by a large creek that ran over countless boulders of all sizes. David looked back realizing they had walked off the road some time before. He wondered how long they had been walking and how far he was from the road. He wondered why he had followed someone he didn't know off the road without even being aware of where he had walked. He was irritated at himself for being so lost in thought that he had not paid attention.

He surveyed his surroundings now. He looked around to see if he could catch a glimpse of the road. The bushes were thick beside the path they were on. Tall trees were interspersed amongst them and lined the creek on both sides. He could hear the birds singing to each other. A bee buzzed loudly as it passed him and landed on an overgrowth of jasmine crawling up the side of an old gate. It sent a whiff of perfume into the air.

Multiple shades of green danced through the leaves of trees and through the grass. A breeze blew off the creek providing relief from the sun. The swimming hole was obviously deep and unusually placed. The creek was shallow and clear, fed by a small waterfall. It flowed over rocks and boulders rippling and playing a strange melody. Birds were dipping and gliding in rhythm with the creek. The creek was silver with little, white ripples. The boulders and rocks were various shades of brown, gray, black, and white. The swimming hole was strangely colorful next to the plain earth tones that fed it. The sky was bright blue with a few wisps of pure white clouds floating high and distant. The blades of grass fed by the ground waters surrounding the creek were refreshing after days of the waving, yellow, dry grasses in the field.

The farmer lifted his tan, muscular body out of the pool on strong arms, and then pulled his dripping body up onto the bank. He shook his black locks that were now straightened from the weight of the water. Curls claimed their original place as the water was tossed with few more head shakes and a squeeze from the farmer's hands.

Although he still stood at a distance, he could make out the strength of the lines of the farmer's arms and back as he put the plaid shirt on over his wet body. He picked up the pair of gloves and placed one hand, then the other, back into their care. Leaving his shirt open, he picked up the straw hat that had been tossed on the bank and sat it on his head. He leaned over, picking up his boots and carried them to a large gray rock. Sitting down, he placed his feet into his worn leather boots and carefully restrung the eyes, tying them loosely.

David watched from a distance suddenly realizing he was just standing there staring. He had not even had a swim. He shook his head in an unconscious response to his own strange behaviors. He had followed a complete stranger into the woods, unaware of where he had gone off the road or how far he had walked, lost in his thoughts. He had stood at a distance watching the farmer swim, get out, and get dressed without ever jumping in and enjoying the refreshing-looking pool. He stood there wearing dirty jeans and shirt, his face and hands darkened by the sweat and dust of the lane.

"You going to jump in, Friend?" David could imagine the familiar grin and twinkling eyes laughing at him even though he was still staring at the back of the farmer's head.

David didn't answer. He walked over feeling very childish again. He sat down just a distance from the farmer as he pulled off his shoes and jumped off the side of the bank. The pool's water was not as cold as he had expected it to be. He was ready for the cold to hit him, but it didn't. It was cool and refreshing, but not cold. He decided it must be the depth of the pool soaking in the warm sun that defied the cold water running over the boulders.

He dunked himself under the water after being sure he was far enough away from the stranger that he could feel safe in doing so. He came out of the water shaking his head as the farmer had previously done. Checking his surroundings once again, he went under hoping to relieve his dirty hair of some of the dust. He shook it again and went under a third time. He swam around for a while enjoying the water. He went under a fourth time, forgetting to look around first. When he came up, the farmer was nowhere to be seen. David searched the surroundings wondering where he had disappeared to and why.

There had been no conversation between them during this whole experience. Still, David felt the farmer should have said he was leaving or something. He got out of the water wondering if he was going to show up suddenly. He waited for what seemed to be an hour or so.

He wasn't sure if he could find his way back out to the lane. He wasn't sure how far he had followed the farmer. He had a small hope that the farmer might show up with some lemonade or sandwiches. He wished he hadn't thought about living off the land. Maybe God thought he was being ungrateful by thinking such a thought. Maybe God had been providing for him through this farmer and he had cut off his own provision by complaining about not living off the land.

His mind was wondering again. He was half-thinking and half-talking to God. “Wish He would just show up,” he thought for the hundredth time since he had begun this journey. “God wouldn’t be mad at me for just thinking about it. He’s not like that. I was just thinking anyway.” His thoughts were racing. “You wouldn’t be that petty, would You?” David was directly talking to God now.

Again, he wasn’t expecting an answer; but also, he was again disappointed that none came. He got up and put his shoes back on. His clothes were still wet and the breeze was cooler. He began to walk back down the path through the bushes and came immediately to the lane after a few yards. David was surprised how close the pool was to the lane.

“I must have only been thinking for a few minutes,” he thought. Just as he started to step back onto the lane, he noticed that the bushes he had walked through were loaded with berries. He reached over and picked one. “Hope this isn’t poison,” he said out loud. He ate the one berry and stood there looking at the rest. It was very sweet and he was hungry. He pulled his wet shirt off and filled it with berries. He decided he would take them with him and if he didn't get sick from the one berry, he would eat the rest in an hour or so.

He shook his head smiling at himself again. "How am I supposed to live off the land if I don't know what to eat or what not to eat?" he asked himself. He walked back down the lane to the fence post. He was carrying his papers since his shirt was wet from his swim. He didn't want to sit in the dust with his wet pants; so, he crossed the lane to the field and found a good spot in the yellow grass to rest. He welcomed the hot sun now as he dried.

He opened the papers and studied them again. Once again, his mind began to race. He lied back holding his wet head on his hands. He closed his eyes and began to imagine what could happen if he was right about speed and time. What if he could really make a motor that had such capacity for speed and continual output? What if he could actually have a vehicle like the one in the drawings he had found? What if he could puncture time or travel faster than the speed of light? What would be the purpose of trying?

David woke up after dark. He sat up and looked around. The shed was behind him looming over him in the light of the few stars out tonight. He realized his back was itching and irritated from the dry grass. His shirt was next to him still filled with berries. He did his best to wipe his back off and scratch where he could reach. He picked up the shirt and headed toward the shed. The shed door was already open when he reached it. He walked carefully through the threshold straining to look around the room as he entered. He could see the desk and the cot.

The window above the desk was just barely visible. He stood there hoping his eyes would adjust. After several minutes, he walked inside and sat on the cot. He opened his shirt and ate every berry until he felt full and satisfied. He was finally living off the land and it didn't taste so bad either.

David lied down on the cot. He found it difficult to sleep since he had napped all afternoon. He stared at the dark above the cot. Something felt different in the room. The door was open and a breeze was coming in the shed. He wasn't sneezing. His nose wasn't running.

"Maybe I am building immunities to mold," he thought. He couldn't remember if he had shut the door. He wondered if he had and if it had opened again on its own. He got up and walked carefully to the open door. As he reached to close it, he saw a strange outline outside to the right of the shed. David caught his breath! He was not able to move! His heart was racing again. He consciously slowed his breathing and thought, "I choose not to be afraid." He hoped that his theory about fear being a choice was true. He had said it many times to other people before this journey.

Yet, he had experienced so many moments of fear the last few days. His heart was still racing. He still didn't want to look to the right. "Fear is a choice. I do not choose it." He spoke out loud again. He had hoped saying it out loud would work. He was still scared. Try as he might, he was having a difficult time proving his own theory.

Finally, he turned to see the shadowy figure outside the shed. Adrenaline was pumping at his temples. The throbbing slowed as he realized the form was not moving. It was too big to be a person or any animal. Whatever it was, it was lifeless. It was just an object. He tried to remember if he had seen it on any of the other nights.

David left the shed and walked into the dark night toward the object. As he got closer, his heart began to race again. This time, it raced from excitement not fear. He held out his hand to run it along cold, hard metal. The few stars that lit the sky gave the metal just enough illumination for him to see and feel that the object was the vehicle from the drawings in the shed. It appeared bigger in person even though the dimensions had been easy to read and understand. He continued running his hand along the metal toward one end.

Suddenly, there was a huge opening. David stopped and felt inside. He could feel a seat. His heart was pounding. Instead of getting inside, he continued walking around the pointed front end, and then started down the other side, walking all the way around the vehicle until he reached the opening again. He stood there at the opening, feeling inside. He ran his hand up and down the back of the seat, and then along the side and bottom. He felt around inside and found something to hold onto and pulled himself up and into the vehicle.

Carefully, he sat down, and then relaxed back into the seat. He moved around to make himself comfortable. Then, vividly aware of his racing pulse and fast breathing, he reached out in front of the seat to feel around. There was a panel and buttons. He lightly drew his fingers across them, being careful not to push any. He counted the number of buttons and calculated where each one was located. He reached to his side feeling first one lever and then another, moving slowly and carefully afraid he might trigger something.

He had forgotten everything he had been thinking or feeling up to this point. He was completely mesmerized by what was happening. He was actually *in* the vehicle from the drawings.

Again, he gingerly felt the buttons, wondering what would happen if he pushed one. What was the worst that could happen? Even if something really bad happened, he would probably find himself waking up by the lane in the morning. This was probably a dream just like the shed. "But, not like the papers." The thought shot through his mind like a knife searing reason and understanding. "And not like the pencil," he thought out loud.

He laid his head back with a heavy sigh. He wasn't sure what was real anymore. In the matter of only a few short days, David had lost his usual ability to think he had a handle on what was truth and what was not. He valued truth. He chose to speak truth, even at his own hurt at times. He read, thought, and searched to discover deep truths. He had taken this walkabout to delve deeper into that discovery; and, in just a few short days, he had lost his ability to know what was real or not real.

He had decided to take control of his life and search for answers to his questioning heart. Now, here alone on this journey, he realized he had less control of what happened to him than he did before. In fact, he had no control at all. He felt a tear at the corner of his eye. It slowly traced a line down his cheek. He had not cried in a long time. He wanted to cry right now. He felt extremely sad and tired. He had known he was sad before. He had known he was tired. This was different. He was feeling his sadness. He was feeling his tired soul. It was not just a physical awareness or an intellectual understanding. He was feeling somewhere he had never let himself go.

Tears filled his eyes, stinging them, inviting him to feel even deeper. One by one, they fell out until he found himself leaning forward with tears falling fast and hard. His shoulders were shaking. His heart felt hot and his emotions hurled out as if vomited from somewhere deep in his gut. Stabbing pains seared though his lungs as his tears fell faster and he broke into a full cry, sobbing uncontrollably. He had forgotten that it actually hurt physically to cry. His chest hurt. His heart was burning. His stomach felt knotted and his head felt heavy and dizzy as he cried harder and harder.

He wanted a deeper truth. He did not want to feel unsatisfied any longer. He was not willing to just settle for each day coming and going without anything changing or feeling important. He had been patient. He had waited. He had trusted God to come to him. He had prayed and read the Bible. He had been faithful to church and to youth group. He had chosen to give up his own rights and everything he felt kept him separated from meeting with God intimately.

He had made difficult choices, feeling lonely and empty to the depths of his soul, refusing to feel sorry for himself or give into his own desires. His desires had actually changed. A new desire to be God's friend had consumed his thoughts and actions. He wanted to be the best friend God ever had. He had been determined to find a way to accomplish that. This walkabout had been his way of trying to experience God.

He had given up all comforts. He had walked away from the hugs of his mom. He had left behind the fellowship of father, brother, sisters, nieces, and nephews. He had left behind the few friends he still had after changing his direction in life. All this had been done to show he really wanted to find God, to discover truth, to become God's friend, and to spend time with Him.

"I failed," David cried out loud. "Here I am worse off than ever. I am hungry, more alone, and more confused than ever. I don't even know what is real anymore. I have completely lost my sense of reality. I'm stuck on some lane afraid to leave and go any farther. I failed trying to find You already! I know less than I did, not more." He cried even deeper. The pain was searing in his chest.

"No wonder I quit crying," he thought. He had cried so much in his life before he quit crying altogether a few years ago. "I forgot it hurts. It hurts so much." He dropped his head in misery onto the panel in front of him onto a button that moved at the weight. The opening was instantly gone, filled in a split second by a sheet of metal closing so fast that David had no time to respond. He was closed inside the vehicle! He sat up quickly, pushing on the door. It appeared to have become a solid piece.

He held his breath. Slowly, he pushed a button in the dark, hoping it was the same one that closed the door. There was no sound. The door didn't open. A light came on and he realized the light was outside the vehicle coming through windows in the front and on the door. He had not felt the vehicle move, and still felt no movement, but as he looked outside, he saw he was in a bright light and there was nothing, or everything, moving. He wasn't sure what he was seeing. It seemed like movement without moving, traveling without change. David drew in a breath and sat back.

Chapter 2

A few seconds passed. He leaned forward to look at the panel, now illuminated by the light through the windows. It was brighter than day outside the vehicle and very light inside. The buttons were in clear view. He leaned closer to look at the glass that surrounded them, startling backward instantly and reaching to touch the beard he had seen in his reflection. His face was covered with hair as if he hadn't shaved for months. His skin was wrinkled and aged. Only a few minutes had passed.

Now, he was sure this was a dream. Feeling quite sure he was safe and would wake up in the morning by the lane, David reached to push a button. Instantly, he felt his stomach turn just a little and his head felt dizzy for a second. He looked outside the window. It was still bright outside. Everything had changed. The vehicle was sitting in the most beautiful surroundings he had ever seen. David smiled, deciding he was going to enjoy this dream since he was stuck in it anyway. He pushed another button and the steel door disappeared, leaving an opening for him to get out of the vehicle.

His feet hurt and they tingled as he moved them. He had to wiggle them and rub them to get them to move. He was stiff and sore. He had to use his hands to lift his legs one at a time to the side and out of the opening. David tried to jump out by pushing himself up and over through the opening; but, when his feet hit the ground, pain shot through his legs. He crumpled to the ground with a groan. He sat back and rubbed his legs and feet for several minutes. Once he was able to stand, he stretched slowly, feeling he had been sitting in the same position forever.

He looked around, trying to understand where he could possibly be. He had never had a dream like this. It didn't feel like he was dreaming. It seemed real. In fact, he was aware that his surroundings felt more real than things felt when he was awake. He was surrounded by trees, flowers, gardens, and grass that had a different hue of green than he had ever seen. In fact, he wasn't sure if it was green at all. He bent over to touch it. The blades moved before his fingers quite reached the ground. He jerked his hand back. "What the…?" He reached out again and the blades moved again as if they were reaching back at him.

"Wow!" He whispered. He touched the blades and they leaned against his hand as if he were magnetized. He pulled his hand away slowly and the blades released his hand. He touched them again and they reached to grip him. He held his hand in place. To his great surprise, the blades began to caress his hand! They were as soft as brand new baby grass. Each blade was perfect, shiny, colorful, and even. He sat down and the blades around his legs and feet began to move in caressing movements. A breeze that felt strangely cool and warm at the same time rippled across his face and down his shirt. He looked down to see his shirt moving in and out as the breeze moved around inside it. It was a rhythmic, repeating movement, making the shirt look like it was dancing on him. He touched it lightly, letting the shirt move against his hand. He could hear birds and insects all around him. It sounded like a strange, beautiful chorus.

He sat quietly, watching the movement of the grass as it caressed him, feeling his shirt dance against his body, and listening to the natural world singing in harmony to the movements. All around, birds were dipping and dashing in rhythmic ballets on the breeze. He could see gardens filled with flowers he had never seen before, boasting indescribable colors and shapes. He watched as they swayed in gentle movements nodding and waving their scented song along the breeze, filling his nose and lungs with aromatic ecstasy.

The trees were joining the garden dance in huge sweeping motions, one by one. They were too big to be moving in response to the gentle breeze. They were dancing on their own, as if they were alive. Joy was filling every cell in his body. He had never experienced a feeling like this. If this was a dream, he never wanted to wake up.

He thought he could hear the echoing of a distant voice singing and stood very still to discover the source of the song. He began to walk in the direction of where the sound seemed to be coming from. He walked through gardens on a narrow path of golden sand lined by pure white stones. Each stone was perfectly rounded although they were different sizes. He knelt down to look at one, picking it up carefully rolling it in his palm. It was about three inches across. The stone look strangely like a pearl. He picked up another, rolling it around. He touched it with his fingers feeling the smooth surface. “Yes, a perfect pearl,” he whispered. David put the pearls back in their places, using his hand to push himself up off the path. He started to brush the gold dust off his hand when he suddenly realized that was exactly what it was!

As the dust fell off his hand to the ground, he was sure he heard a small child-like giggle. He looked around, seeing no one. Still amazed at the gold and pearls, he walked closer to the voice that was now growing louder. He walked around a slight bend in the path through some large fruit trees that seemed to move a little to make more room for him to pass. The voice slowly became a gentle roaring sound. As he turned another bend, he saw a waterfall rushing down a tall, rocky wall into a pool of deep, green water. As he stepped off the path onto a lush green bed of grass, the blades wrapped his foot in caressing touches. He moved closer to the emerald pool.

At the bank of the pool, David knelt and looked down into it. The reflection made him jump. Staring back at him was the clean shaven face of a much younger David with someone leaning over him.

In one quick motion, David touched his face and looked behind himself. There was no one there. He looked back at his reflection. His face was clean shaven. The beard and older, sun-wrinkled face that had been reflected back at him inside the vehicle had disappeared. First, he had been older and now, he was younger. He noticed his hands were very young with smooth skin.

He leaned back over the pool. Gazing to its bottom, he could see its bed was lined with millions of emeralds glistening in the clear water. There was still someone else with him in the reflection. The ripples in the water distorted the face of the person behind him. He jerked his head around as fast as he could to catch the person standing behind him. There was no one there. Again, he stared into the pool. Then, he turned his head as slowly as possible; and still, no one was behind him even though he could see someone in the reflection.

David's own eyes were staring back at him from his reflection with the same wonderment he was feeling, wide green eyes of a younger David. They seemed to be asking, "Hey, what in the world is going on?" He felt like he should answer. "Okay, now I am really losing it!" he thought, but still he answered the eyes in the reflection. "I have no clue!"

He watched the reflection of his lips move, and then saw his mouth begin to smile. He started to giggle, and then he broke into a hearty laugh, falling backward onto the caressing grass as he shouted to the lost reflection. "Now that is the ultimate experience of talking to yourself!" He laughed at his own joke and at the feeling of joy that kept surging through his being. He laughed till he was tired, lying still in the grass enjoying the massage of the blades stroking his forehead. He closed his eyes, his long, dark lashes lying against his cheeks. Suddenly, he opened his eyes and sat up. There was no way he was going to fall asleep right now! He didn't want to wake up on that dusty lane by the dry grass field feeling lonely, lost, and unsure. He loved being here wherever it was. If it was a dream, he would make it last. If he was awake, which seemed to be the case, he had traveled to some place or some time that he didn't want to leave! Just being here made him feel happy. His tears and anguish which had seemed only moments ago were forgotten. The fears he had recently experienced were gone as well. In fact, he realized he had no negative feelings at all!

He looked around wanting to take in every detail of this place and engrave it in his memory should he wake up or find himself somewhere else. In front of him, the huge waterfall towered over the pool spilling its silvery, frothy wetness into the deep, green water. David estimated it to be at least 100 yards high above the pool, which was probably 100 yards across and more like a small lake. It was flowing in a circular, bubbling motion. The roar of the waterfall sounded like a deep voice. He closed his eyes again, leaning his head back trying to see if he could make out any words. "I am…" The voice wasn't really clear. Maybe it was just his imagination and not a voice. "I am…" He couldn't quite make it out.

"I am what?" David asked out loud. "Now, I am taking to water again!" He shook his head and smiled, helping himself up to his feet to look around. The grass grew right up to the edge of the pool and down into it. The gold path also went right down into the pool, as did the row of pearls lining it.

The grass was still except for the blades now caressing his feet. The flowers in the perfectly manicured gardens were still dancing with the trees. The breeze blew through his shirt, causing his shirt to move again. Strangely, he felt as if he were a part of his surroundings.

Three birds were flying directly in front of him about a foot from his face. Their little eyes were gazing into his as they flew closer.

He reached out, expecting them to dart away. Instead, they lit one by one in a perfect row on his arm. All three were looking directly into his eyes. Each was a different color and shape. Their feathered bodies displayed colors that were similar to salmon, gold, amber, turquoise, deep garnet red, emerald green, and some colors he couldn't come close to naming.

The salmon-colored one had a unique crest of pure white feathers on its little head. Its beak was as bright as a red ruby. Its little amber eyes shined and winked at him.

An amber-colored one with turquoise speckles and a bright gold beak gazed at him with shiny, emerald-green eyes. A deep garnet-colored one, slightly larger than the others, stared at him with gold eyes. Its white beak reminded him of the pearls lining the lane. All three perched on his lifted arm. He held it there, not wanting them to fly away.

Finally, he lowered his arm slowly bringing it closer to his face. The birds held their perch and continued to gaze at him, breaking into the most harmonious and beautiful song he had ever heard. They sang to him for several minutes, and then flew off to one of the gardens at his left, closer to the waterfall. Their song lost its volume, becoming one with the roar of "I am…, I am…." from the waterfall.

David walked back onto the path and followed it back to where he had first discovered it. He looked around at the trees. He had never seen such trees. Their roots were mostly up above the ground. It appeared as if they were standing on several legs. Their branches were dancing. As he watched, they seemed to be moving as if they were clapping in time to the voice of the waterfall, the songs of birds, and choir of insects filling the breeze with melody.

Everything seemed to be alive. "Not just alive," he said, "alive, like me." As he spoke out loud, the trees all made a bow in unison and the grass blades lied flat as if a wind had suddenly blown through the scene. David was amazed. He spoke again out loud, “Alive, like me.” They bowed again. He smiled and said, “Like me!” Again, he got the same result. Every few minutes, he experimented with the discovery. “Like me,” he would say, or sing, or shout all with the same effect. Nature responded.

The strange vehicle that had brought him here was gleaming in the center of a grassy field. He walked back to it and looked into the space where he had sat before. He didn’t want to get in. If he did, it may close on its own and take him somewhere else. He was not ready to leave here yet.

He looked around at the buttons. He walked around the vehicle several times feeling the hard shiny metal, looking for an opening that could reveal its source of power. It appeared to be solid. He knocked on the front with his knuckles, noting it wasn’t solid. Instead, it had a slightly hollow sound. He looked again at the buttons. There were strange drawings carved on each one. They were symbols of some kind that David had never seen before. He stared at each one for a few minutes trying to figure out what they might indicate.

He wanted to look closer, but would need to get in to do so. He was not ready to try that. He walked around the entirety of the vehicle again, wondering if it were possible that the motor he had designed would work in it. It was definitely the same vehicle he had seen in the drawings from the shed. The only difference was the lack of an open and empty compartment for a motor.

Obviously, the motor was already in the vehicle. He wondered if it was his motor. Of course, it would be if this was his dream. Again, he had that strange feeling that this was not a dream. He was awake. He was more awake than he had ever felt.

"Of course, I could be dreaming that, too," he thought out loud. He reached up to touch his smooth face. "It has to be a dream. I couldn't wake up younger." His eyes were filled with the wonderment he was feeling. He smiled, rubbing his hairless chin.

"Unless," he thought out loud again. He looked back at the vehicle where the motor would be and surveyed his surroundings He looked at the back of his hands. They were very young looking, but still as large as they were as a man. He looked down his legs to his feet. Yes, he was still as tall and his feet were still as large as they were before. He was obviously younger looking, but not smaller. "Unless," he whispered.

David thought about the trip in the vehicle. It had seemed like a few moments. He had begun as he knew himself: 24, 6' 2", with a goatee and mustache that had been unshaped or trimmed for a few days. He had seen a reflection of himself in the vehicle with a longer beard and a lined face. He had ended up with no beard at all. All this had occurred in just a few moments. Or, had it? Had he traveled to another place, or had he traveled to a different time? Or, had he done both? Or, was he dreaming? Could this all really be happening?

He ran his hand along the metal once again. He sat down with his back against the vehicle and closed his eyes. He was tired, deeply tired. Although he hoped he would not fall asleep and wake up on the lane again, he kept his tired eyes closed. Falling into a deep sleep, he dreamed of tacos and his niece running to him after she got home from daycare. Even in his sleep, a faint smile crossed his lips in response. It is nice to be loved by the innocent who only see the good in you.

He dreamed of the beach and ocean waves slapping onto the sand. He dreamed of the sunny Sunday afternoons with his family after church. He dreamed. Suddenly, David jumped, awakening, expecting to find himself by the lane.

He looked around in amazement at a flock of birds sitting on a small tree branch right in front of him. Strange creatures were grouped around him. He looked behind himself to see if he was still by the vehicle. He was. The scene was till the same except for the small birds on the small tree and the creatures staring at him.

He rubbed his eyes. Yes, he was waking up from dreaming. Then, this was not a dream! Could he have dreamed inside a dream? No, he was awake. He shook his head to clear his thoughts, rubbed his eyes once again, and sat forward. He leaned with his chin on his hands resting them on his knees and stared back at the birds, which all responded in different songs.

Then, he looked back at the creatures, one by one. Each responded to his stare with a sound and a movement, until all were moving together in a strange dance. His shirt was dancing from the breeze exiting it to caress his face with finger-like strokes.

The pearls along one side of the path were moving, rolling toward the sound of the waterfall, "I am…." He still could not make out the rest. The pearls on the other side were rolling back as if from the pool. The small tree's roots were all exposed and standing, making David believe it must have walked there.

At that thought, it swayed its branches and bowed as the birds lifted into the air. They swooped and dashed, still singing. The grass had grown around him and was caressing him all along his feet and body. He could feel the gentle touch of each blade along his neck. It caused him to shudder and sent a sense of well-being surging through him. He felt intensely alive. Everything around him was living. Actually, everything was more alive than he had known alive to be before. Trees were free to walk around and move at will. Birds sang in harmony. Water spoke. Grass could respond and move on its own. Wind had life. It was as if they had all been set free from natural laws as he understood them.

He ran his hand on the metal of the vehicle as he stood beside it. He looked at it as if to apologize for not continuing its inspection or discovery. He really didn't care how it worked right now.

He started down the path toward the pool, hearing the waterfall as he walked closer. "Hi," he said to the rolling pearls. He wasn't sure if he expected them to respond, but he was sure that they could hear him.

Just before he got to the pool, he saw that there was a path that veered off to the right. He hadn't noticed it before. "If it was there before," he thought out loud.

He stepped over the rolling pearls onto the new path, which was strewn with seashells of all sorts and sizes. Interestingly, they didn't crack or break under his weight. He realized he was barely touching them. In fact, it was almost like his steps were just above them, as if he were gliding along. He lifted his right foot high, bending his knee. He felt strangely light, but stable. He lifted his other knee and didn't fall. He was floating above the path with both knees and feet off the ground. He stretched out his legs behind him, leaning forward.

With a shout of excitement, he began moving himself over the path with his arms. He wasn't actually flying. He was suspended mid-air rowing himself along with his hands. He began moving his legs like a frog to move faster. He laughed. He couldn't help it. The sound of laughter was all around him.

Birds were circling him. Creatures were running, flying, and jumping around him. New creatures joined in the crusade. A flying lizard with eyes that protruded on long tentacles and circled around in all directions like a ball bearing flew next to his face, chirping in a giggling sound. One of its eyed tentacles stretched toward him taking a closer look at David's face.

A dragon fly with a metallic turquoise body and transparent rose-colored wings buzzed past him, followed by giant insects that looked like little, gray-spotted horses with white manes and silver wings. Tiny translucent human-like creatures with pointed ears and pointed, stiff, orange hair sat on their backs.

Several dark blue disc-like objects spiraled around his entire body from his head to his feet as they moved past him. They looked like sand dollars, with hundreds of little feet that moved them along through the air. Small white eyes circled the discs, opening and closing one at a time making them look like white, blinking lights. One turned as it passed him, displaying the flat upper side of the disc. Etched into its surface was a beautiful, flowered design.

Three large creatures flew straight at David and hovered for a few seconds, and then they began moving backwards in front of him as he stroked his way along. They had round white bodies that turned in a circular motion above six golden wheels all going in different directions at the same time. They had heads that circled in an opposite direction of their bodies. As each head turned, David saw each head had four faces. Each face was a different color. Each face had one eye, an up-turned nose, two pink cat-like ears, and rosy pursed lips. They looked like they were ready with a kiss on each face as the heads turned around and around, each eye looking at David in its turn.

He laughed as he rowed himself along above the shell path. The creatures were making whirring sounds as they turned and each face giggled with a different sound.

After several yards, he lowered his legs to walk again, enjoying the light floating feeling and the breeze now flowing through his shirt again in dance-like movements. Farther down the path, David could hear the sound of children laughing and talking. Excited to see another human, he hurried to a run, gliding just above the shells.

Ahead of him, there was a grove of trees. Each tree was covered with beautiful flowers of different colors. He could smell their fragrance as he came closer. The creatures all moved off toward the trees, disappearing through the branches and flowers. Then, the wind brought the waft of a sweet scent. It smelled like a mixture of strawberries, melons, and oranges.

When he reached the first tree, it bowed displaying its strange fruit growing out from the centers of large, fragrant ivory blooms. The fruit was oval with a smooth skin and a color he had never seen before. It was a strange hue of turquoise pearl glazing over a ruby red. He reached to pick it and it dropped into his hand. He bit into its fleshy meat. The taste was unlike anything David could describe. It reminded him of honey and cream with a hint of vanilla, cantaloupe, and apple. In fact, it was similar to the taste of fruit salad when you get a huge bite of everything all at once.

The laughter of the children grew louder and filled the air as he moved along the path through the trees. The leaves in the branches were stirring in a sound much like the laughter. Just past the fruit trees, David stepped out onto a sandy beach covered with children. Some were running and laughing. Others were intent in giggles and conversations playing in groups. The entire beach was covered with children of all ages. As he walked onto the beach, he realized the sand on the beach was shining and clear. He picked up a small handful and let the diamond-like sands run through his fingers. He picked up another handful to inspect them closer.

"Diamonds," he whispered to himself, looking up with the diamonds still in his hand. The beach seemed to go on forever. As he walked through crowds of children, some would come up to him, touch him, and dart off giggling. A small child came up to him and stood in his way, causing David to stop. He looked up at him with clear blue eyes, his blonde hair glittering like the diamonds. He stood there looking intently at David, who was looking back at him and feeling a strange tug in his gut. "Hi, little guy," he said kindly.

"Uncle Bubba?" the toddler asked. David felt a mixture of wonder and love surge through him. Uncle Bubba was what his nieces and nephews called him.

"Uncle Bubba?" shouted another little voice as another small child came running up. David looked to see a small brown face with deep dimples, green eyes, and curly, dark brown locks. The two toddlers took hands and stood looking at David together. David got down on his knees and looked directly at the two little toddlers. "Hi, I'm Uncle Bubba." It was said as more of an affirmation than an introduction. The two instantly hugged him, and then ran off holding hands and laughing. David couldn't help following them through the crowd. They looked back every now and then as if to make sure he was still coming.

It seemed the crowd of children went on forever until the beach suddenly ended as unexpectedly as it had first began. In front of him, there was a vast ocean as smooth and clear as a sheet of glass. He could see right through the clear, smooth water as if it were not even there. Every detail of life in the water was clearly visible, colorful, and alive. He wished his mother was here with him right now. How he wished she could see what he was looking at! His mother loved aquariums! Here was an ocean aquarium clearly visible and full of the most amazing water life you could imagine for as far as his eye could see, which right now was much farther than he understood seeing to be.

The two children he had followed stopped at the edge, looked back, and then ran right into the ocean. Involuntarily, his hand reached out in a gesture to stop them, then fell at his side as he watched them continue running in the clear ocean along its white, glistening bottom until they were engulfed and completely under water, still running together on the bottom, holding hands, and looking back every so often. The dark curls and soft blonde locks floated in the water around their faces.

Another older youth he had seen at the edge of the beach was suddenly right beside him, looking into his eyes. As he took David's hand, he gave a little tug. "Come on!" The cherub-like voice sent thrills through him. The voice was so strangely familiar, as were the amber-colored eyes ever so slightly slanted upward. Yet, he was unable to identify exactly what was so familiar about them. The youth's face was ruddy and beautiful, surrounded by curly dark locks.

"Come on!" The youth's command was expectant and inviting. David ran with him, following the toddlers into the ocean. They ran along the sea floor. He could see clearly and was breathing, or at least he wasn't drowning. He wasn't really sure what he was doing. He knew he was still alive. He was running along the bottom of a sea, covered with water so sparkling clear and smooth, he could see the birds flying above the water's edge. He could hear them singing.

Nearby, whales joined in calling in a gentle, low song and swimming in to circle around the toddlers as they continued to run to and fro between coral reefs and schools of unimaginable fish. He could see large octopi with long, flowing arms moving at a great speed through the distant plant-like structures on the far left side of the sea, closer to the beach. He was sure they must be at least 25 feet long unless the water made them appear larger. Three of them moved together through the distant, dreamy landscape.

David could see some older children enter the water farther down the beach. He watched as the octopi swam past them. They grabbed the tentacles of one and held tight as the giant creature pulled them out into the forest of plants and beautiful fish, swimming them through leaves and sea flowers.

An enormous sea turtle paddled past the children through large yellow sea plants, gliding through the sea in an opposite direction. David saw the children let go of the octopus and grab the tail of the turtle. They pulled themselves up onto its back and lied down holding the shell as it carried them back to the beach, where it walked them up and out of the water.

David and the youth ran through a school of bright blue and yellow fish. Instead of swimming off, they began circling David's arms and legs brushing his skin with their stiff scales. He ran on, still following the toddlers deeper and farther out on the diamond floor of the vast sea. Huge fish came and circled the runners.

David's pace automatically slowed as his friend ran on ahead. The fish were several yards long. Black and silver stripes ran along each fish from head to tail. The blue and yellow fish swam off and began to brush the large fish circling their huge bodies in a spiraling school. Then, as if by a silent signal, the school swam off leaving David face to face with the large fish. They moved in and bumped him gently, nudging him forward.

He began to run again and soon caught up with his friend, who had stopped several yards away to watch an enormous manta ray gently fly by. David couldn't help but reach out to touch it as it passed by him. The skin was an unusual color. It was almost orange with leopard-like spotting in a dark green hue. Navy blue lines ran along the side and striped the wings. The two toddlers had stopped at a distance and were staring off into the sea, as if waiting for something.

Suddenly, David stopped, feeling his own hair float around his face. His running partner stopped with him to watch a most spectacular sight. The two toddlers opened their arms wide and with hands clasped, they stood still. Coming at full speed from a distance was a creature so awesome and so large, it seemed to stretch the distance of half the sea, for at least as far as was visible to David. Its head seemed as long as a city block. The eyes were as red as flames of fire. The body of the creature was dragon-like with fish scales as large as a door. Each scale was as brilliantly white and luminescent as a perfect pearl. Its head surfaced above the water and David could see its red eyes blazing. It opened its nostrils as huge orange and yellow flames shot into the air causing laughter to explode from every child on the beach.

Again, the creature sent flames into the air in colors of pinks and blues, causing screeches of delight that pulsated through the waters. A third time, flames blew high into the air in the most brilliant fuchsia and purple. This sent ripples of songs, dancing, and clapping through all the beach onlookers. The creature ascended out of the water in a slow and steady leap into the air so high, he was able to do a complete flip in the air and descend in a steady, smooth dive back to the sea floor and toward the spreading arms of the toddlers.

Letting go of each other's hands, they grabbed a welcoming wing-like fin and held on as the creature swept them onto its back, carrying them deeper and farther out into the clear sea. David stood still, unable to do anything but watch with the deepest joy he had ever experienced up to that moment. He began to laugh. He was laughing under water!

David could see the creature returning through the crystal water, gliding effortlessly past whales and under dolphins that scooted along the surface on their tails. The dolphins flipped in huge circular dives above the length of the white glistening scales of the creature gliding along on beautiful, almost translucent, glass-like wings, or fins. He wasn't sure which they were; but, they were beautiful and graceful and carried the creature smoothly through the water directly in front of him. The amazing head and eyes were so large! David couldn't move. He just stared at them. The toddlers slid down the wings to the sea floor where they began to run the length of diamond sand at its bottom toward David.

The creature ascended up and out of the water with one smooth movement carrying it into the heights above the trees and beyond. He watched as it gracefully ascended back into the sea at a great distance, miles away. The toddlers held hands and walked along the floor of the sea with David and his young companion back toward the beach.

David looked back, imagining what it would be like to ride the creature himself; yet, unsure whether he would like it once it carried him deeper into the depths of coral and seaweed. He could only imagine what intense creatures he might face. He decided he would come back sometime and try it if he could.

The toddlers led David and his young companion up and out of the water and onto the beach of diamonds. The rest of the children were gone from the beach and all was quiet except for the music of the birds and gentle calls of the whales somewhere in the depths of the sea. Their music blended in gentle harmony with the secret song of the wind playing continually in the background. The toddlers rushed away in excitement. The little towheaded toddler stopped and ran back for a quick hug at David's knees and a deep look into his eyes.

"Love you, Uncle Bubba," he whispered and turned to run again. He was not as swift a runner as the other toddler, who slowed to allow him to catch up.

The young companion stayed with David. He was quiet as they walked along. There seemed to be no need for words. Both David and his companion were comfortable with just each other's presence. David guessed him to be between 15 to 18 years old. He was handsome and strong-bodied. Muscles rippled in his calves as he strolled just slightly ahead. His gait was strangely familiar.

"You hungry, Friend?" he asked David. The young boy's amber eyes twinkled as if teasing him. "You hungry?" asked his companion again.

David didn't know if he was hungry or not. It sounded fun to eat though, so he nodded. The young man broke into a jogging run and David matched his step. He was long past even trying to figure out what was going to happen next, where he was, why he was here, or how long it would last. He was just lost in the experience, enjoying every moment he could and expectant for what might come.

The toddlers disappeared into a garden and the young man slowed to a stop at its edge. He sat down wrapping his arms around his legs and resting his head on his knees staring off at the sea they had just left. David sat next to him and followed suit. They stared for a long time. The quiet was not uncomfortable. The young man was clearly enjoying the sight as much as David was. He felt he could sit here forever and watch the beautiful sea, the playing dolphins, the whales surfacing, and the swooping and singing birds all framed by the beach of glistening diamonds and the rosy, glowing atmosphere. The water itself appeared to be a mirror of the birds above and a clear glass to peer through at the same time. It was almost too beautiful to take in; and yet, one couldn't help but try to do just that. The beautiful, white sea creature was nowhere to be seen. Still, David held the memory of his presence vividly and dreamed of riding through the sea as the toddlers had done today.

"He is quite handsome, isn't he?" asked the young companion as if reading David's thoughts.

"Very!" was all David could respond. He noticed that the young man was holding a basket out to him. "Where did that come from?" he thought to himself. Inside the basket, there were biscuits similar to the ones he had experienced before. These were perfect in shape, smooth and round, perfectly golden. David tasted one, only to discover the taste of honey and butter much like the biscuits he'd enjoyed beside the lane, only even more delicious.

The young man offered David a drink from a flask of hammered silver and gold. It was patterned with a beautiful engraving of grapes and a sword.

David took a long drink of the juice. It reminded him of pomegranate and grapes, yet sweeter and thicker than what he would expect. The young boy smiled and took a drink himself. They sat for a long time, enjoying the biscuits and juice and gazing at the beautiful sea. In the background, David could hear the echo of the waterfall, "I am…" and the harmony of the wind and birds. The air was perfect and the light was rosy and glowing. He was sure he had never felt as good as he did at that moment.

Chapter 3

David sat up, realizing he had dozed off. He looked around and could not see his companion anywhere. He got up and began walking toward the waterfall again. He stopped to examine a cluster of grapes growing from a tree. As he inspected it, it dropped into his hand. They were actually more like little red berries than grapes. They almost looked like a cranberry, but were pungently sweet and invigorating. He carried them away nibbling at them as he followed the path to the waterfall.

Suddenly, he realized he was not walking toward the waterfall at all. He could still hear the sound of its waters speaking their mysterious "I am…," but the path had changed. He had turned wrongly; or, maybe he had taken the wrong path completely. He turned to walk back the way he had come and he saw that even the path behind him had changed; and, he was lost in a maze of herbs and flowers on a path that was strewn with soft rose petals of a strange shade of pink. Mixed among the petals were little droplets of red liquid shining in the rosy light.

Small, delicate, white lilies grew just beside the path, standing very still and appearing very reverent. Their tiny leaves seemed to be held in prayerful grace and their small white blossoms appeared to be bowed in silent prayer. David felt awed by the entire scene. He sensed a deep respect in the posture of the surroundings. There was an air of reverence and quiet. David stared at the delicate rose petals, breathing in their fragrance. He had no choice but to walk on the rose petals and tiny red droplets if he moved at all. He stood still not wanting to step on them.

Finally, he took a step. He felt a strange and searing sensation as his feet crushed the gentle petals and the red liquid stained their soft surfaces. The lilies bowed deeper in response to each irreverent step he took along the path. The crushed, reddened rose petals sent out a sweet aroma that rose into his nostrils and filled the air.

David felt an even deeper stirring flooding his soul as he walked on carefully. Tears began falling from his eyes and dropping like crystals along the path as he continued, wishing the path to end. There was no way to avoid crushing the petals or to keep from splattering the red droplets all over and staining the path and delicate petals as he moved. He couldn't lift his eyes to see how far the path would go. He walked and wept along the path. He walked and walked. He wept and wept until his body felt tired and he dropped on his knees, watching the red liquid splash as he did so. He picked up a small handful of petals and let them fall gently through his fingers. As the last red-stained petal fell gently to the ground, David finally looked up from his kneeling position. Directly in front of him was his young companion.

Reaching out his hand to David, he stared directly into David's eyes with his own amber eyes blazing as brilliantly as fire. As they looked into each other's eyes, David felt the tears flowing down his face. He took the young man's hand and the sound of the waterfall echoed loudly, "I am…" The young man helped David to his feet and turned to walk in the direction David had been walking. Trees and flowers rustled as they passed. The path had changed and there were no more rose petals to crush. Instead, gems of all colors covered the path which was now surrounded by various bushes and trees. Each tree had several kinds of fruit and flowers. The bushes hung with huge berries and leaves of different colors of turquoise, green, yellow, flaming red, bronze, salmon pink, bright green, blue, olive, and other colors David couldn't name. The fruit were brightly colored with contrasting patterns that appeared to have been hand-painted. The scents made his heart race with excitement.

When the path suddenly opened up in front of him, David saw a tall, craggy mountain made of shimmering gold with veins of silver running through the edges. It glistened and sparkled with large gems placed in artistic displays of scenic patterns. Atop the mountain, stood a castle made completely of boulders and engraved wood beams, each with different and elaborate details. As they started to ascend the mountain, David began to see the details more clearly. Each boulder was carved with pictures of himself at different ages or of family members. Memories that were vividly engraved in his heart were right there in front of him carved into perfect designs on each large boulder. Each boulder displayed a different shade of green, orange, cream, rust, gray, white, brown, or rose. They were marbled with ivory veins, huge and majestic in size.

He had to cross over a bridge made of gemstones that carried him over a small steam flowing around the castle. The entire bridge was made of emeralds, rubies, topaz, and sapphires. They were as huge as his head. He attempted to see what held them together, but could see nothing. The bridge was gently curved upward and over the water. As he crossed it, he could see that the water below was as clear as glass and the bed of the stream was glistening gold with diamonds, rubies, emeralds, sapphires, and many other gems scattered around. Fish with long flowing tails surfaced and blew bubbles that floated up into the air and off into the trees. He continued across until he came to the castle.

There was a brown boulder carved with a scene of him kneeling by a train track, placing a penny on it to be flattened by a train. Next to it was a green boulder showing him as a young child holding a crawdad. He was holding it up high as if to show someone. His eyes were large with wonder and a smile of delight exposed large dimples. Above that, carved into a rose-colored stone, was a picture of him by a campfire at his Aunt Petey's house as a young boy. He was sitting forward holding a long stick, staring into the fire. He was wearing long shorts and a large plaid jacket hanging open. Above him, the sky was filled with stars.

Each boulder was different, and each was carved perfectly, depicting him at different ages. David stopped to look at one that was unfamiliar to him. He saw himself as a young man. There were several young women. One was looking at David. In the scene, David was dancing with delight on his face, his eyes closed, arms out straight, and hands upturned. As he stared at the carving, he felt a strange shudder run through his body. He felt like he could step into the scene. In fact, he craved to step into it. The feeling was so intense he put his hands out to touch the boulder. He could feel a pulse in the rock. He studied it for several minutes trying to remember this scene. He could not.

The young woman seemed familiar. He felt as if he should know her. He stared for a long time. It seemed like she was looking right at him out of the boulder and into his heart. There was something in her eyes that sent a strange feeling through David's soul. He wasn't sure if it was a good feeling or one of sorrow and regret. He stared for a long time. "Who is she?' he thought. He was sure he should remember. Her eyes appeared to follow him as he moved on slowly, still touching the pulsating stones.

He looked at the next boulder and saw the young woman dancing with arms raised and head back. Her hand was holding a scarf or cloth. It appeared that she was waving it. Its details were exquisite! It had embroidery along its edge that spelled out a message hidden in the folds. David tried to read them, but couldn't quite make out any words. The rest of the material was detailed with a map of some sort. She stood on her toes. Bracelets were hanging on her ankles and from her wrists.

Whoever had carved this boulder had taken extra time in detailing the beauty of each item. Her legs and feet were feminine and strong. Her lithe arms were perfect and defined. Each hair was etched in detail as it touched her cheeks and waved down over her shoulders. So vivid were the details, David once thought she moved.

He was sure he had seen the movement of her hips and feet in dance. It felt like something he had experienced before. He rubbed his eyes and looked again. He could see himself in the scene, in the background among many spectators watching the dance. After several minutes, David moved on. The artwork itself was too much to take in. The attraction of the young woman was mesmerizing. Who was she? He couldn't remember.

Finally, he moved along to another one that showed him reaching out to the young woman whose back was to him as she walked away. David felt a strange feeling rush through him. He couldn't shake the feeling and wanted to stop looking at the carving; yet, he found himself unable to move for minutes. Then, he continued on. He saw a scene of the young woman and himself holding hands in a dance. Side by side, with arms lifted and hands clenched, they danced on the top of a jagged ridge overlooking a canyon.

David loved this etching. He loved it in the same way you would love a person. He wanted to hold it, to kiss it, to embrace it, and to never let it go. He laughed. He wept. It made him feel content, fulfilled, and full of a joy he couldn't understand. What was this feeling? He felt like the scene was a memory, yet he could not recall it. It created in him a mixture of excitement and desire, longing and yearning, and comfort and rest.

The next scene was an engraving of David and the young women kneeling in prayer. Again, their hands were clasped and their bodies were leaning against each other, the young woman's head touching his chest, David's head leaning over hers. The artist had engraved it so the bodies were separate, yet one, etched in lines that became unified, flowing together. He felt he could write a poem about this scene. He tried to write one in his head, but there were no words to express what he saw there. Completeness, unity, joy, expression, fulfillment, and love came to mind. Nothing seemed close to expressing what he was looking at or feeling. Up until this moment, David had thought he must be in heaven or at least in the future on earth. The scenes on the boulders before the ones with the young woman depicted his past. All the things around him now were too full of life to be what he knew of earth. Yet, this scene he could not remember. If it was from his past, then he had lost the memory. "Maybe it hasn't happened yet." David startled as the voice spoke to him from the scene itself. The walls began to move as if they were breathing and then they started chuckling.

David took a step back, not sure what to make of it all. The rock had spoken to him!

He looked around to see if the voice had come from somewhere else. Along the top of the castle, thick and heavy wood formed a canopy, marvelously detailed in carvings of cars, geometric designs, faces, and other objects and scenes he remembered to have drawn throughout his young life. Here they all were, etched into a massive dark wood carving memorialized along the top of a marvelous castle.

There were windows that were just openings without glass. Some of them had water trickling down them like open fountains flowing into an open-ended trench made of hammered bronze medal at the bottom of the open windows. The water then dropped to another trench farther down cascading to the bottom into a small stream. It flowed in circulating pools around the edge of the castle.

David circled the castle in wonderment at all the scenes. Before he reached the other side, he came to a very tall, carved wood door. The carving made him stop short. It had been stained with colors and etched with such precision that it was very life-like. It was a perfectly detailed picture of him kneeling on the red-stained rose petals reaching out to take the hand of the young companion. He noted that in the background of the scene there was a cross with a goblet etched on its center, tipped and spilling red liquid from it onto the rose petals. He closed his eyes and wept again, though he wasn't sure why.

David stood for quite a while staring at the door. "Go ahead, it's for you," said his young companion. He had forgotten he was not alone and the voice surprised him out of his thoughts. He was bewildered for a few seconds. "Go ahead!" The young man gestured and commanded at the same time. "It's for you!"

He pushed open the door, which seemed to open more easily than such heavy wood should have. He saw a small wooden table off to the right with a basket and the flask. " I thought you might be hungry, Friend," said his companion. The young man turned and walked away, leaving David inside the castle. He quickly turned to stop him. "Wait," he said as he swung around, only to discover the young man was nowhere to be seen.

He stood just inside the door. It was still open and he let his eyes search the beautifully carved scene of the rose petal path. David loved to carve things himself. The three dimensional perspective here was so precise that the carved bodies of himself, and of the young companion reaching out to him, looked as if any second they would move and come to life. Finally, he turned to inspect the inside of the castle. The carved boulders lined the walls on the inside with even more scenes of David's childhood.

One caught his eye and he moved to it to inspect it closely. It made him smile. There he was as a three year old toddler balancing his pillow, a huge blanket, and a stack of clothes. He remembered this scene. It was the day he had told his mother he was running away from home and she told him he'd have to carry all his stuff if he did. She had carefully piled pillow, blanket, clothes, and whatever else she could find, to make his load very heavy, asking him where he intended to live when he ran away. He had very seriously answered, "Down at the river, under the bridge."

She had asked him how he would eat. He had responded, "Guess I'll eat crawdads from the river." She had continued to question him. How he would survive? With one question after another she laid out possibilities he would face on his own. She ended by explaining to him that if he chose to run away, he could never come back unless he promised never to run away again.

He had left the house piled high with too much to carry and stood for a second outside the back door. He had knocked on the door as if it were no longer his home. His mother had opened the door with an air of unfamiliarity, "Yes, how can I help you?"

He had answered, "I decided not to run away."

She'd replied, "Well, you can't come back now unless you promise never to run away again."

"I won't," he'd said meekly; and then, he'd walked past her with a brief aside, "'sides, there'd be no TV."

David smiled looking back on his mother's wisdom. He missed her. He wondered if she was worried about him and if she was praying right now about his walkabout. What would she think if she knew what he was doing and where he was?

"What *am* I doing and *where* am I?" He thought out loud. He ran his hand along each wall studying all the scenes on the boulders. There was the one of him catching a hummingbird with his bare hands when he was about 11. One of him hanging upside down from a tree he had fallen through. He could just make out a hand holding his foot and the tip of a wing. The entire room was carved boulders.

David realized the floor was clear and he could see right through it. The veins of silver running through gold lie just beneath in beautiful patterns and shapes. Flowers were growing in the clear floor underneath and in whatever substance the floor was made of. "They must be living," he thought. "I can smell them."

One wall had water running like a fountain that fell into a pool so inviting, David looked around and stripped from his clothes down to his underwear. He stepped in, feeling it pulsate and bubble around him. The water was as warm as a bathtub and a sweet fragrance began to swirl around him. He let his head lie back as his body relaxed to the natural massage of the water. He closed his eyes and rested.

When he finally decided to open his eyes again, he noticed that the top of the walls had no ceiling. He hadn't noticed that before. Creatures were peering at him from the top of the room. Leaning over the edge of the boulder wall, they looked at him. He stepped out and put his clothes back on his wet and rested body. He looked up again and they began to laugh. Some sounded like they were speaking foreign languages. Some made clicking and chirping sounds.

None of the creatures were familiar to David. One creature made a descent from the top of the wall utilizing a middle set of wings. It had a total of six wings, three on each side. When it was in front of him, it used the bottom set of wings to stay in place in a swimming-like motion, facing David. It stared into his eyes. It seemed to be gathering some sort of information as it watched intently.

Then without warning, it rose through the opening at the top and disappeared with all six wings rotating in a circular motion, reminding David of a train. Its long tail swept back and forth like a rudder. So swift was its ascent that David lost sight of its rose-colored body and yellow-tipped wings in an instant. Its face had been almost human with rounded cheeks and red, pursed lips. Long thick lashes had edged the brilliant, yellow, gem-like eyes. Its rosy ears were pointed with little wing-like edgings. He hoped it would come back, planning to try to capture it the way he had the humming bird as a child. "Just for a closer look," he thought out loud.

The winged creature was back in a flash. He returned with six fellows just like him. Each was only slightly different in some way. They came closer and stared at him. David reached out fast expecting them to hurry away. Instead, they stayed right where they were as he grasped one of them quickly. The creature's wings stopped. It seemed very content with David catching it.

He opened his hand and the creature stayed with its wings moving again. David held out his hand and the creature sat on it. Two middle wings were moving gracefully and slowly. Its brilliant eyes twinkled and the human-like face actually broke into a smile. The red, pursed lips were now grinning from one winged ear to the other. David studied the creature now perched contentedly on his palm. Still grinning, it stared back.

"What are you?" David asked out loud. At that, all of the little creatures broke into laughter and darted away up through the open roof and out of sight.

Other creatures were still peering over the edge at him. There were a few that appeared very bird-like. They had beaks similar to hummingbirds, long and slender. They were as large as a small house cat. Each had a tuft of golden hair coming out just below the beak and curling into a something similar to a beard. They had tails that were narrow like a mouse with a ball of dark blue fur at the end. Their body and tails were flesh colored. Their eyes were large and metallic red, outlined with a thick stroke of dark blue reminding David of his sister's eyeliner. Their beaks looked like they were made from ivory. As he stared at them, one raised its head and let out a melodious flute-like song. At this, the other creatures joined in with a harmony of sounds filling the air.

There were some similar to monkeys. They had large wings, as translucent as cellophane which spread about a yard across. Their faces appeared young and innocent, with large dark eyes and long dark lashes. Their bodies had no hair except for a small white crest on top.

David stayed for what seemed like hours staring at the different creatures and wondering where on earth he was. He wondered if he was even still on earth.

He finally walked to the entrance and looked around again at the boulders the scenes from his life. Wherever he was, he knew it was meant for him to be here. That gave him a feeling of indescribable peace.

He had expected adventure on his walkabout; but, he had never dreamed of what was actually happening to him. He wondered if anyone would ever believe him. He questioned if he would ever be able to tell anyone. He wondered if he had left behind his past and family forever. He walked aimlessly thinking and wondering until he finally sat down at the foot of a tree.

He laid his head back and closed his eyes. He thought about the machine that had brought him here. He thought about the reflection of himself with a long beard and how he now appeared very young with no facial hair. He thought about the shed in the field and the farmer that kept appearing with food. He thought about how he would fall asleep in the shed and wake up back on the dusty lane.

He looked around at his surroundings; and suddenly, he jumped up and began to run, once again feeling himself running just above the ground. He wanted to feel the ground under his feet. At that thought, his feet hit the ground and he ran at a pace too fast for a man to run. He felt energy pulsing through his body. As he ran, large creatures joined him from the surrounding trees. A lion twice the size of any lion he had ever seen was at his side keeping pace. Leopards, tigers, elephants, horses, giraffes, zebra, deer, buffalo, and others began to emerge from the surrounding plant-life. They ran in pace with him. They were so large he should have been afraid. Instead, he felt energized as he ran with them. They veered off as he turned an unfamiliar bend off the path.

David continued. He felt no fatigue or desire to slow his pace. He soon found himself in the middle of a crowd of people. Children, youths, babies, and young adults all stood in a large crowd watching him approach. He stopped as suddenly as he had started and stood looking back at them. Creatures of various sizes and shapes, all very large, stood among the crowd. They had a translucent glow that made them seem more like mirages than something solid.

He stood for a moment taking it all in, then leaned back his head and sang out, "Like me!" The crowd cheered. The creatures glowed brighter and broke into singing, and all around nature responded in sounds and movement. When David let his head drop back to see the crowd, they were gone and all was quiet except for the distant sound of the waterfall whispering, "I am…"

He looked all around, hoping to see a creature or a human. He wanted to talk with one of them. He wanted conversation and explanations. "Hello?" It was weak and so he shouted again. "Hello?" He heard rustling, a whisper, and quiet laughter.

"Hello?" He smiled. Again, he heard the rustling and strained to see where it came from. Uncertain, he tried again. "Hello?" This caused giggling and whispers all around him. David sat down. He stared into the growth of bushes and trees. He caught a glimpse of movement by the tall root of one tree. He kept his eyes averted, using peripheral vision to watch for movement. He saw none. He turned to the right, catching the swift movement of a child darting between bushes. He looked directly at the bushes and couldn't make out any more movement or see the child. Out of the corner of his eye, he saw a creature fly from one limb to another in a tree.

"Hello! I see you!" He smiled again. Laughter broke out and birds sang loudly as several children ran out from the bushes. Others began to appear, dropping out of trees on branches, hanging on knees upside down and laughing and talking in strange languages. The large translucent beings began to appear out of thin air becoming more and more visible.

"Hello!" David was almost shouting. In one musical sound, the creatures all around him sang out, "Hello."

"Where am I?" He called out. They moved in closer in one unified movement.

"Here!"

After a second or two, David laughed.

"Where?" He sang out loudly with a forced vibrato as if singing opera on a stage, amusing himself purposely.

"Here!" The crowd sang back, accompanied by an invisible orchestra of instruments.

David stretched his arms out, stuck out his chest, and threw his head back, singing loudly. "I like it here!"

The orchestra of instruments sounded and trumpets blew as the crowd hummed a note and all of the natural wildlife around him bowed in slow motion. All bowed except the young companion who suddenly appeared out of the crowd, walking toward David with a dimpled smile. His amber, almond-shaped eyes slanting even more with the white-toothed grin on his tan face.

David walked toward him. He felt like playing. "I like it here!" He sang with a forced and playfully deep bass.

The young companion sang back in like fashion, also with a playfully deep bass and an exaggerated vibrato. He then began to dance in a playful step twirling and jumping, bowing and dipping. David couldn't help himself. He began to dance and jump around as if he were in a ballet. He sang in strange and unusual, exaggerated tones. His young companion was accompanying him as they both delighted the crowd of witnesses with their playful abandon. Some were laughing with joy and clapping. Other creatures hummed background music. Trees were dancing and their branches were clapping. Birds were dipping and whistling.

Out of one side of the crowd, several young men appeared cartwheeling and back flipping in gymnastic prowess, joining the two entertainers. Suddenly, from their midst a young man appeared. His dark curly locks framed a rosy-cheeked face. His eyes were as dark as ripe olives. He bowed to David's companion who was still dancing. The young companion reached out, joining hands with the beautiful young man. Their feet moved together in choreographed perfection. The young companion held out his other hand for David to join. He did. To his amazement, he realized he was mimicking their steps perfectly and with ease. They were no-longer just playfully entertaining the crowd. They were amazingly dancing with such beauty and grace, the crowd of witnesses sat together in one movement to observe. The music rose to a crescendo, filling the atmosphere with glorious sounds as more large, translucent beings appeared, filling every empty space and bowing on one knee with hands raised.

The dance continued until another young man came spinning and dancing from the crowd. His skill was mesmerizing. His dark face and eyes were very child-like though he was every bit as tall as David. He joined the three, grasping David's hand. They all danced together with abandonment and delight. The young dark man let David's hand drop and began to dance in front of the other three dancers. He was breathtaking as he moved. He danced with grace and ease with a child-like smile and wide eyes. David continued to dance but had forgotten himself or his own movement as he watched the thrilling display of the young man.

His dark face was contrasted by the most beautiful, white teeth in a full-lipped grin that seemed to be innocent and teasing at the same time. His curly locks were pulled back and banded in the back with a cord of gems that glistened in competition with the sparkles in the young man's hair, some of which had fallen out of the band and hung loosely framing his face and falling over his eyes.

There was something very familiar and adoring in the way he tossed them from his face every now and then. Once, he brushed a lock from his eye as he came down from a beautiful leap, with a graceful sweep of his hand. The move was so familiar to David he missed a step and almost tripped over himself. Why couldn't he remember? "Who is he?" David was trying hard to remember. His face was so familiar! The movements held a secret place in David's mind.

The young man leapt again high into the air, lifting his bent legs up behind him. He leaned his head back and in the air his body formed a perfect "O" in the movement. As he straightened out and came back to the ground with his feet touching as lightly as a balloon, he gave a familiar nod toward David. With a wide grin, he tossed the fallen curls from his face and danced back into the crowd with his feet moving so fast and smoothly, they seemed as if they did not quite touch the ground.

David smiled remembering for just a second who this was. Then, the memory faded and he stopped dancing wishing to remember. The tug on his other hand caused him to begin dancing again as he looked into the crowd searching for the young man. Once, he caught a glimpse of his face and almost remembered again.

Soon, others joined the three dancers one by one. A group of young women with tambourines moved to the front of the crowd led by a very young boy with bouncy, golden hair. He was dressed in a wrap of pearl white satin. "Dance, Uncle Bubba," he laughed. The tambourines all shook at the same time and David could see bracelets of bells wrapped around the wrists and the ankles of the dancers.

As the dance continued, children came out of the crowd. They began to sing to the orchestrated music. Their beautiful young voices were so musical they were like melodious instruments. They were singing in a beautiful and strange language. David closed his eyes, sang, and danced.

Suddenly, he realized he was no longer holding hands with his fellow dancers. He opened his eyes to see all had stopped to watch him. He turned to look into the eyes of his young companion. He could see approval and love in the amber eyes. David experienced a sense of the acceptance and belonging he was always looking for. He loved back like he had never loved before.

He stopped dancing, dropped his hands, and then in playful abandon, sang out a finale, "OH yes…….I like it here…………" The last note held for several seconds with strong, exaggerated vibrato. Again, the crowd laughed and clapped in applause as David bowed in a playful gesture.

The young companion patted his back and threw his arm around him as he led him off toward a grassy knoll. They walked silently with warm and happy smiles.

David and his companion sat for hours chewing on blades of grass. David talked off and on sharing things he had held in his heart over the years. His companion listened, turning to look at him every time he talked.

Now and then, the companion responded, showing his interest. David shared deep things, unusual things. Sometimes, the companion would speak, but mostly he listened and looked at David with heartfelt respect and love. David loved this feeling more than anything he had ever even dreamed of feeling. He had so many questions he could have asked in this moment. Strangely, he did not feel any need for answers to anything. The experience itself was more than satisfying. Just being was enough, being here with this friend.

He was deeply moved. He felt complete, whole, real, and satisfied. He felt like he could stay with this new companion forever and never need anything else. Finally, he felt like he knew what it meant to be completely understood and still be accepted and respected. He knew what it felt like to be known and still be totally loved, without fear. Indescribable joy and freedom overcame him as he shared and shared, knowing his companion cared about what he was saying. He shared deep secrets he had feared to voice before. He felt no judgment. He emptied his heart.

He realized that this friendship he was experiencing was even closer and more wonderful than any relationship he had known previously. It was more real and fulfilling than being with any girlfriend, being with his siblings, or even being with his mom or dad. He felt he could live forever with nothing else than this bond he felt. "I like being here," he said in a whisper to his friend.

"Me, too." The answer was louder than David's, but was spoken with deep emotion. "I have longed for today, for this moment."

"Me, too," David realized he had copied his friend's answer.

Then, "Well, I didn't know that I longed for this. I mean… I longed for this feeling, or something. Whatever I have wished for so long…well, forever, was this….this," he was repeating himself. "I mean..."

"I know. I know you, David."

"That's what's so cool! I can feel that. I can feel you know me and….well, and you still like me." David smiled and chuckled slightly in a self-searching recognition of why he had just said that.

"You still like me in spite of knowing me." This time it was said with a deep sigh.

"Actually, I not only like you. I really love you, and..." the pause was brief. "I care about what you think. I am interested in you and your thoughts. I always have been." David glanced at his young companion at the last statement. The young man smiled and looked back. "Yes, always have been."

He then lied down on his back and picked a blade of grass chewing on the end as he closed his eyes.

David sat for a while. He wasn't sure what to say right then. He knew that his thoughts had often been something he would not have wanted to have this friend know he was thinking. It sent an involuntary shudder through him. He wished he could go back and undo some of his thoughts, erase them, and think differently. He wished he could go back and choose to think only what he'd want to share with his friend. It felt so stirring to be loved and respected. He wanted only that right now. He knew his life had been filled with undesirable thoughts and actions. He wanted to weep. He wanted to weep so hard he could wash away all he had ever done so he would never have to feel any shame with this new and loved friend. It felt too good to feel respected. It felt too wonderful to feel heard and loved at the same time. He wanted to be clean completely. David closed his eyes and lied down. As his body touched the ground, he could hear a slight crushing sound. He felt a silky softness as if he had lied down on a deep pillow and his body was becoming warm as if a bath of warm water was engulfing him.

He opened his eyes slowly wondering what he was going to see now. He could see he had lied down on a deep blanket of rose petals. Warm red liquid was oozing out of the petals he had crushed and was running all over his skin, staining it red. He turned quickly in surprise. The young companion had turned to look at him, the blade of grass still between his beautiful white teeth. A red tear was dropping from his eye. It fell onto the stream from the petals. David looked deeply into his companion's eyes. He loved those eyes. The expression in them was searing. They began to blaze like fingers of an amber fire shooting out toward him. David felt burning sensations throughout his entire being.

Again, the need to cry himself clean overcame him and he let out a sound that came from somewhere deep within. Rain began to pour like buckets on him. Water was hitting him in drops as big as cupfuls. It poured over him, cooling the burning fire that was surging through him and washing away the need for tears. David and the young man continued to look into each other's eyes. He emitted another sound like a deep and emptying sigh, glad the young man was still there with him.

"I never leave you, David. I am with you always. Be confident of that." David let out another sigh and closed his eyes to contemplate what was just said. The water stopped. David's eyes opened quickly. He was lying on grass. His companion was nowhere to be seen. The crowds were gone. The music had stopped. All was very still. David felt weightless, as if the weight of his body had been removed.

He looked around realizing that he had somehow arrived back at the vehicle. It had changed dramatically. It was glowing like the translucent creatures. The smooth metal sides were gone, replaced with a gem-like substance that looked like diamonds, yet felt like liquid or gel to the touch. The door was missing.

The gel–like substance was moving as if it were breathing. It seemed alive and welcoming. Inside, the panels were lighted and glowing. Gold and silver had replaced all the metal inside. The seat was made of thick, soft fur as white as wool. A gentle tune came from inside.

He moved closer to get inside, deciding that he could easily get out without any doors to close. As soon as he sat, a translucent film covered the entrance and the sound of thunder shook the vehicle as it bolted like a streak of lightning, leaving David surprised and breathless. He desperately looked at the panels and buttons wanting to push something to stop this machine from taking him away.

He felt a deep longing, a sad yearning tearing at his heart as he felt the machine taking him away from the place where everything lived and responded. It was taking him away from the friend he had discovered and the fulfillment he had enjoyed. It was sweeping him away from respect, belonging, love, joy, acceptance, forgiveness, and all the fullness he had always wished for. It was taking him away from everything that could ever matter again.

Chapter 4

He was afraid to push buttons; yet, he felt desperately that he had to. He could see his reflection in the panel as he shouted, “Stop!” His face looked sad and desperate. His eyes were filling with tears. His reflection began to fade and he could no longer see himself in the panel. He looked down at his body and realized he could not see himself at all. He lifted his hand to look at it, but saw no hand. He tried to touch his face. There were no hands or face or body. Yet, he could feel himself there. He was existing and alive, but his mortal being was gone. He was there and not there. He couldn’t push a button if he tried. The vehicle had stopped anyway although he hadn’t yet noticed, so busy he was with the discovery of his body being absent. The translucent film was gone.

Eventually, he moved to leave the vehicle and found he was outside of it as instantly as his thought to leave it had come and gone. He tried again to see or feel himself and couldn’t. He gazed at the surroundings. It appeared that where he stood was very similar to where he had just been. Maybe he was still in the same place. Maybe he’d stopped the vehicle in time. His thoughts were racing.

“Where am I? Where is my body? Did I kill myself by stopping the machine? My body is gone. I can still think.” He was talking out loud to himself again.

The grass was green. The sky was a brilliant blue. The trees were moving, as alive as before. Even the grass was moving and the same gentle tunes of wind and birds sounded around him. But, there was something very different. The ground was wet and a warm mist was rising all around him, filling the air with moisture and warmth. Plants were very green and healthy. Trees were extraordinarily large. They had the same roots above the ground. David could see gardens of flowers and fruits trees all around him.

He heard the giggle of a female in the distance, then laughter. Out of the trees, a young woman ran with raised arms and a bright smile. She stopped and turned in a circle, swaying like a dancer, and then fell backwards without a care onto soft, thick grass. David wasn't sure what to do. She hadn't seen him. He was invisible to her.

Suddenly, a young man broke through the garden into the open field looking around. The grass was so thick the man could not see where the young woman was lying. In his hands, he carried a wreath of flowers and a huge cream-colored melon. He let out a whistle that reminded David of a bird. David heard a muffled giggle.

The young man heard it and began to move stealthily in its direction. Suddenly, the young man pounced into the grass and the young woman screamed in delighted surprise. The two sat up and broke into laughter completely unaware of David's presence. David realized that neither of the two had any clothes on. He stared and thought it was the most beautiful couple and scene he had ever witnessed.

The young man was lying on his side, half sitting now. His body was muscular and defined. The color of his skin was an olive-toned brown. His hair was dark brown with a copper highlight that shined as he tossed long waves off his handsome face. His teeth were white and straight; and, his smile was broad in full lips. His cheekbones were high and defined. His eyes were almost yellow, the irises lined with black, matching his pupils and long, curled lashes. His eyes were oval, slightly almond shaped. His eyebrows were dark and thick with an upward sweep in the center that gave him a look of alertness. His cheeks were round and his face was strong and muscled.

David was not sure what nationality he might be. He looked slightly like a Pacific Islander, maybe Asian. His features were broader though, more like an African, as were his full lips. When David searched his profile, he decided he could actually be Caucasian with darker skin.

The woman sat next to him, leaning back on him with her head resting on his shoulder, her long and silky hair flowing across his arms and chest. The waves of her dark hair ended in loose ringlets at the ends. It was beautiful, almost the color of dark chocolate highlighted with an auburn-bronze when the sun hit it just right. She was even more difficult to define. She had a light olive complexion, more beautiful than any David had ever seen. Her nose was perfect. It was straight, just slightly upturned, and just broad enough to be beautiful. Her lips were as full as the young man's. Her eyes were almost a turquoise green with brown flecks and black-lined irises. Her lashes were long and dark. Her eyebrows were perfect, lining her beautiful eyes in the same oval arch and slanted at the ends like her eyes. She too could have been Caucasian, African, Asian, Latin, Egyptian or a mixture of all. What a beautiful and perfect blend of all nationalities they displayed!

The man broke open the melon. She took a bite, and then held it to the young man's mouth as he took juicy bites letting the juice run down his face. He playfully picked up her hair to wipe his chin.

She laughed and took a handful of melon and rubbed it on his face, jumping up and running off again. He was up as fast, catching her and wrapping his arms around her. He held her close, kissing her with his lips and face still wet from the melon. They took hands and walked back into the trees, swinging their arms together like children.

David felt a surge of mixed emotions. He felt he had intruded upon something very intimate and private. He had been enveloped with the sensation of beauty and innocence and had not been able to turn his eyes away. He felt a deep loneliness and surging desire. He spoke in a pitiful tone. "Oh God! I am so alone!"

He started to cry in deep sobs. He felt the sadness rolling through him. He reached up to touch his eyes and wipe any tears away in the same manner that he was accustomed to doing.

In a shocking revelation, he remembered he could not feel his body or see it. There was nothing to him. He had no substance at all. He was entirely sadness and loneliness, confusion and desire. He was nothing but feelings and thoughts. The feeling of loneliness grew deeper as he realized he didn't even have himself.

He couldn't sit or move or touch. He was not even there; yet, he was. He knew he was there and knowledge was all he had. Knowledge of his sadness, his indescribable desire, his guilt for staring at the young couple, his sorrow, and an urge to scream for help! And, that he did! "Help! Help! Help!" He repeated it louder each time and with more desperation. "Oh, God! Help me!"

Suddenly, he began to see his body. It was more like an apparition than a human body, but it looked like his arms and legs. He could see right through himself, but he could still see that he was there and that helped. "Help!" He shouted again with just slightly less desperation.

"Come, walk with me, Friend!" The familiar voice startled David as he turned to look at who had spoken to him. There was no one there. "Come, let's walk." The voice was moving toward the trees where the couple had disappeared.

"Where are you? Who are you?" David asked.

"I am right here with you."

"I can't see anything. No one is there."

"Are you there?" asked the voice.

"What? What do you mean?"

"Are you there? You can't see yourself; but, are you there?" David was confused, but still got the point. The voice was so familiar.

"Come walk with me!" It was more of a command than a request. David hurried to stay close to the voice. His loneliness had vanished and he surely did not want it to return.

"Where are we?"

"We are right here!" the voice laughed.

Suddenly, David heard a small squeal and the young woman came bounding through the trees. "I heard you walking!" Her voice evidenced the delight. "I could hardly wait any longer! Come! See the man! He has given me something beautiful!" The young woman wasn't looking at David, but at something right beside him. He looked down and could still see his translucent self.

"She must not be able to see me," David mused.

"What has he given you?" asked the voice with true interest.

She pushed back some beautiful flowers along the way as she walked into an open space beside a beautiful waterfall. There lying on the ground was the wreath of flowers that the young man had been carrying. "He made it for me," she said in childlike abandon. "Isn't it beautiful?"

"Yes, very!" said the voice. "Here he comes now."

The young man came through some bushes and leapt up on a boulder with one foot, bounding down again into the open space where they stood.

"I heard you!" he said with the same child-like delight as the young woman.

David was silent as the three of them conversed, once again feeling like an intruder.

"Come walk with me," said the voice. David followed closely behind as the couple walked with the voice and carried on a very intimate and loving conversation. They talked about the things around them and how delightful they were. They showed off some new fruit bushes they had discovered, telling the voice how good they tasted.

They walked through beautiful pathways leading through gardens of several varieties of flowers and bushes. David spied a berry bush and reached to grab a few. His hand went right through the bush, or maybe the bush went right through his hand. Either way, he was unable to procure any berries.

They continued to walk and talk for hours. David followed silently, wandering through the warm mist rising thicker as the sky grew rose-colored. David stopped to look around and get his bearings. When he turned back, the couple was gone.

"Where did they go?" he asked, expecting the voice to answer. There was no answer. The sky was growing darker. David could hear wild sounds rising out of the mist. He was sure he heard a roar of some wild beast in the distance and the cackling of a troop of primates somewhere close by. Low-throated calls came from every bush and grew louder as the mist thickened and the night grew black.

David looked around to see if there was a place to shelter for the night. The sounds of night animals grew louder. The mist grew thicker. He couldn't see more than a foot in front of himself. The damp mist was not affecting him physically. He looked down to see his translucent outline. He did not have a physical body for the mist to get wet or cold. The two people had not been able to see him and he hoped that would be true of the animals as well, should any come his way.

He wondered around in the mist for what seemed days to him. He wished for the voice to speak to him. Twice, he called out in a weak whisper to it, hoping he would get an answer and not alert any beasts of his location. The noises around him grew louder as he walked. Some of the sounds were so close; he felt he must be next to them. It was too dark and misty to see anything at all. David realized he could be walking right through great beasts and not even be able to feel it. After all, when he'd tried to touch the fruit, his hand had passed right through it. He didn't have a body.

He began to sing in a whisper. As he grew braver, his song became louder. The eastern skyline began to lighten. He sang louder as the sky grew rosy and the sun came up. Dewey grass, dripping trees, and flowers were the only evidence left of the great mist of the night.

The sounds of the animals had grown quieter. There were still sounds of birds and primates. An occasional soft roar or howl could be heard not far from where he stood.

As he walked through the flowers and bushes, he was amazed at how groomed and beautiful they seemed. He saw no dead leaves, only vibrant healthy plants and grass. The trees were amazing and brilliant.

David thought of his mom and her love of flowers and plants. He wished she was there to see the beauty of this place. It was obviously well cared for, perfectly planned, and designed by some master gardener. Everything was healthy and placed in groups and gardens that formed combinations of designs and colors his artful eye could appreciate. Each was a well-planned garden. Each had a design and composition that took his breath away.

He spent hours wondering around and enjoying the colors and scents. He was startled once by a group of beautiful tropical birds. Brilliantly colored parrots at least three times the size of any he had ever seen had flown right through the trees landing in the great branches of a towering tree. There, they conversed in beautiful conversations that sounded very human-like, but in a language strange to David's ears.

He came upon a pond with graceful birds that reminded him of swans. They were much bigger, though and resembled peacocks in coloring. The pond had strange lily pads with blue flowers much like blue morning glories, but big and full. Even the pond and lily pads appeared to be carefully planned and designed. The flowered lily pads were grouped in sets of three. Around the pond, there were groupings of different grasses. Some were tall and reminded David of the pampas grass that grew so beautifully in his coastal home in California. These were much healthier and their colors were more vibrant with no evidence of dying leaves or stems.

One group was purple and yellow. Another was lime green and scarlet red. One was pink and cream. The fourth was blue and gold. One group was planted for each side of the pond. The lime green and scarlet was on the eastern side. The pink and cream was on the south end. The purple and yellow were on the west, and the blue and gold on the north end. In between each group, there were smaller grasses with beautiful furry, white heads.

A flock of white geese and seven shiny ducks landed on the pond at the same time. A huge flock of small multi-colored parrots flew past David, singing and chatting to each other and disappearing into the trees. Several large birds that seemed to float more than fly gracefully landed next to him, walking on tall crane-like legs. They had long, flowing white feathers on their scarlet heads and long, flowing white tail feathers. Their bodies were a dark, gleaming emerald green. They had thick yellow lines that seemed to be painted around their dark eyes like eyelashes. Their beaks were curved and onyx black. They walked with a graceful stride, their tails resembling a bridal gown behind them. The long white feathers on their head seemed much like a bridal veil as well. "Bridal birds," thought David out loud.

Other birds began to show up singing in the trees and bushes, filling the morning air with beautiful and peaceful sounds that soothed David deeply. He was filled with peace. He felt rested and unafraid. He could hear laughter and began to walk toward the sound. He wondered through several carefully designed trails and under beautiful trees with giant fruits.

He suddenly came upon the source of the sound. The young couple was sitting against a tree trunk eating a fruit of some strange color. He looked at the tree and saw that it had several different kinds of fruit. He could count 12 different varieties. The couple still did not notice him. They sat laughing and talking for hours completely lost in each other's conversations and looking into each other's eyes, often leaning their head on the shoulder of the other. When they finally stood up, David moved closer. Still, they did not recognize he was there at all.

David followed the couple throughout the whole day, watching them walk through herb gardens, smelling different flowers, and greeting many different animals. Some were so large that David couldn't believe the gentleness they displayed. Tigers, leopards, and panthers with silky patterns and brilliant eyes brushed against the couple for attention. Their long fangs glistened as they appeared to smile and respond to the touch of the young man's hands, growling and rubbing against him for more. Smaller versions of wild cats lazed on the lower limbs of trees purring and licking their fur in contentment. The young man stopped here and there to caress the beautiful patterns on their sleek bodies.

The young woman reached to touch the points on the long tufted ears of a sable-colored kitten lying beside its auburn mother. It had lime green eyes with dark rims. The mother had the same dark markings and brilliant eyes. The tufts on their ears were as black as the lines that surrounded their slanted eyes.

The kitten yawned, displaying strong, white fangs and a pink tongue that curled as it stretched outward and upward in slow motion. It stretched its body to full length and let its claws grow in the stretch. Then, it sat up and began to lick its paws and use them to wash its own face. The mother cat leaned in with a stretch of her own body and a few licks of her long tongue to aid in the cleaning process. It rubbed its eyes and face against its mother's tongue, and then turned on its back in another lazy stretch while the mother continued to bathe her baby. The purring grew to a soft rumble as the two harmonized in lovely sounds of companionship and contentment.

Several unique creatures came in and out of the bushes to receive loving touches from the young couple.

A white wolf at least twice the size of any David had seen sauntered up and circled the couple, rubbing them with its soft, long white fur. Its glowing, yellow eyes closed in ecstatic response as the man ruffled the wolf's neck and leaned in to give him a hug and a nuzzle on his cheek. The wolf's wet, red tongue licked the side of the man's head in grateful thanks and reciprocated love.

Throughout the day, creatures came to get a touch from the couple. Some were so different from anything David had seen, he couldn't even name any animal similar to them. He wasn't even sure if they were animals at all.

A group of creatures came through the trees on white feathered wings. When they landed next to the couple, they were very human in appearance, except for their skin, which was almost pearl and translucent. Their white hair was long and wavy with curly ends. Their voices were like glorious songs and when more than one talked at once, their voices harmonized. The winged creatures rose just above them, waving their wings. It was unusual and beautiful. It seemed spontaneous and choreographed at the same time.

More creatures floated into view joining in the chorus. The sound of the crowd's wings became a roaring wind causing the trees to wave and bend in the breeze. The leaves of the trees rustled louder and louder until they too sounded like an instrument. The limbs began to slap together and the leaves rustling with the clapping of branches rose to a crescendo of applause.

The animals began to howl and sing. David noticed rocks cracking in a sound of cries, opening to display treasures of diamonds, opals, and crystal. Insects and winged birds were buzzing, tweeting, and whistling in harmony in the background. Everything seemed to be in unity. David felt that he was a part of it and a song began to burst from him involuntarily. Somewhere in the distance, he heard the sounds of trumpeting and bells. The whole world was singing and David's involuntary song rose louder.

> "I am His. He is mine. He has loved me all this time.
> I know him. He knows me. This is how it was meant to be.
> I cannot but praise, His anthem raise. In unity as nature plays

His glorious song.
I need it now. And all day long.
To hear the voice all day, all night
Is my desire. Is my delight!
Come heal and seal! It feels so real.
I love you. You love me. Come now, feed me.
With your words. With your breathe. You give me life. You stop my death.
I want to love! I want to give! Keep me alive! I want to live!"

The day passed quickly and soon the sky began to turn a deep turquoise with a gold and salmon glow. The sounds of moving leaves and rustling bushes began to raise a new sound. The breeze was scented with evening mint and lavender. The smells and warm glow in the heavens sent a wave of peace and joy surging through David. Contentment welled up from a hiding place in his spirit, pushing past any tired feelings of discontent and forgotten wishes and daydreams. What was here right now felt good enough. Nothing was needed. Nothing was missing. All was good. It was very, very good!

David heard a strange sound coming from somewhere in a growth of trees and flowers. The couple heard it also and jumped with delight, grabbing each other's hands and running toward the sound. David followed. It sounded like water in a brook. As they got closer, it sounded more like a waterfall. David slowed as he began to hear the familiar sound of "I am…" and then, the sound became a voice speaking. "I am here!" It was the voice he had been longing to hear all night and all day.

The couple began to dance like children holding each other and twirling around till they dropped with exhaustion. Then, they got up still holding hands as they began to talk and the voice answered. They were telling the voice about all the things they had enjoyed that day. They were asking questions. The voice was giving them answers. They turned their heads as they spoke and it seemed as if they could see who they were talking to.

David ventured to interrupt at one point when there was a moment of silence. "I missed you and was hoping you would come back." The couple could not hear him. The voice responded.

"I am here. I am always with you. Be confident of that." The couple did not seem to notice that the voice was now talking to David. He felt something like electricity pulsing through his body.

"I am glad you are here! I love you!" David felt like a child. He couldn't help saying it.

"I love *you*!" The voice responded causing David to begin to weep with ecstasy and joy.

"Okay, so I am real though. I am here even though nothing can see me and I don't have a body?" He just had to ask.

The voice laughed with joy and spoke kindly, "Yes, you are real. You are here because I am thinking of you. Your body is not here because you are not real in the way you understand. Your ways are not my ways, though. The way you understand things are not the same way as I understand them. My understanding is unsearchable."

"Then, I am not here and I am not real. Am I dead?"

Again, the laughter came. "You are not born yet."

"I can see a form of me."

"Right now, David, you are my thought. My thoughts are as real as my words. You are as real as you will always be."

"I don't understand."

"I know. I told you that already."

"I thought I had left you or you had left me. I can't see you. I can barely see me."

"I am always with you."

"I know, you said that."

"You do? You know that?"

"Well, I believe it. Does that count for anything? I don't ever want to lose how you make me feel." Even saying it made David shudder with its revelation. Nothing could feel this complete and joyful.

"Do you understand how it feels to me to be accepted and completely loved like I belong to something or someone?

Do you know I have been desperate for someone that could fill my heart like this? I know that sounds strange. I don't even care right now that it is just a friendship. I kept looking for it before. I wanted to find my, well… my soul-mate or something. I wanted a wife. I wanted to love and to be loved so badly, it was eating away my very soul!

Do you understand that having you as my companion and friend filled something in me?

Do you understand that I don't care how strange that seems, even to me? I love you and I need what you fill in me. Even if I never have anyone else, I can't be without you. I need what you give me. I can't lose you. Do you understand that?"

David realized how desperate he sounded. He didn't care. "My heart is desperate for more of you, more of your voice. I can't wait to hear it. I want to see your eyes again. I want to see you look at me!"

Even as he said it, David could hear the sound of the waterfall in the distance growing louder, "I am…" A form took shape in front of him and David could see glowing eyes and a strong, beautiful smile. The eyes looked deeply into David's.

"Let's dance!" The voice was speaking as the translucent form of a man began to glow. The young man and woman responded to the voice and began to dance in circles around the translucent form. The voice began to sing as the form danced in abandonment with the couple, and soon David joined in even though the couple could not see him.

The song was deep and moving with a lilt that made it light and free at the same time. The voice sang,

> "Come away and dance my friend, come sing and dance with me.
> Come play and talk the nights away and live forever free.
> You say you cannot be without my friendship or my voice.
> I feel the same and long to hear you praise me by your choice.
> I made you good, yes very good. You fulfill my heart's desire.

I want your heart for me alone, consumed
with passion's fire.

How can you love without that love that's
burning deeply now?

How can you fill another's heart when yours
is unhealed somehow?
Take this love you now know. Let it
consume your soul.
Then, it is yours to give away and make
another whole.

Passion burns with passion's fire. It cannot
flame alone.

When you are filled with passion's fire, it
melts your heart of stone.

Why give a stone instead of flesh that's
healed enough to bring
What you have found in me alone. It will
cause your heart to sing.
A singing heart is one to share. You must
make sure you give
To one who shares the passion fire or passion
will not live."

The sun dropped suddenly and the evening came to a close as a thick mist began to grow around him and the couple faded from his view.

"Hello?" It was a desperate cry. No answer came and David knew that the voice would not be heard again till the next day. He wondered around in the mist for the night thinking about what the voice had said. "I exist before I am born? I exist because he has thought of me. I am a thought. His thought, so I am real. Wow!"

David didn't stop moving the entire night. He walked. He thought. He laughed. A few times, he cried. He wanted to hear the voice again, even just one word.

"So, I am obviously in the Garden of Eden and I am watching Adam and Eve. My mom would give anything to see this!" He was talking to himself just to hear a voice. He felt strangely lonely. It was a deeper feeling than being lonely. There was a hollow place deep within his being, a void that yearned for the voice. This desire was stronger than any description David could come up with.

"Yes," he thought out loud, "it is like being in love, yet even more than that." Even the physical desires he had experienced could not compare with the desire to hear the voice of the one who's very thought of him made him exist, the one who had brought him into *being* with a thought. To know that this someone had desired him enough to create him and to think him into being filled a place that had been unfilled his whole life.

David had always longed to feel desired, to feel wanted, and to feel important. The realization that someone powerful enough to make him exist had wanted him to exist was overpowering. Yes, it was deeper than being in love. It was deeper than wanting to be in love.

Morning came and the mist was warmed with sunshine. Sounds of the night grew quiet and birds began to sing. The air was warm, moist, and clean. Scents of fruits, flowers, herbs, and spices were carried on the breeze. David could not imagine anywhere more delightful. He watched the various and unique birds and creatures throughout the day. He wondered through orchards of trees and smiled at huge creatures that towered above some of the smaller trees.

One creature especially attracted David's attention. It was at least twice as tall as a giraffe, standing on huge back legs. The pattern on its skin was very similar to a python, yet with emerald and bronze scales that glistened like metallic art. It had small front legs with claw-like hands. Its eyes were piercing and black when it swung its head around to return attention toward David. It had been walking in the same direction as David and had slowed, allowing him to get closer.

Its towering head was small at the end of a long neck. It looked very much like a dinosaur in shape, yet very snake-like in coloring and patterns. Without turning its body, it swung its head around and down facing David eye to eye with piercing dark eyes that seemed to shine with intelligence and a knowing that caused him to shudder.

The beauty of its skin was incredible and detailed. David was mesmerized. He couldn't move. The eyes looked into David's as the head moved closer almost touching his face. It tilted its head in speculation, and then unfolded two large wings that had been folded against its body in a camouflage of patterns like the skin, except transparently thin.

This startled David, yet his body only flinched. He was unable to move. After a few moments that seemed like hours, it swung its head around and continued down the path, leaving David standing in the same spot. David was still, realizing the creature could see him. It was a strange moment in this beautiful place of peace and fulfillment. The creature was so beautiful and moved with such grace for its size that David was unsure of why he had felt the intimidation and fear that had seared through his soul. "It could see me!" He whispered hoping the voice would hear him and come to his aid. He desired the comfort of the voice more than ever.

After several minutes, David was able to move. He wasn't sure if he wanted to follow the same path since the creature had moved that way. His feet began moving and he found himself walking forward.

David heard a giggle, then a man's voice. It was the young couple. He took a few steps faster toward the sound. Suddenly, he stopped short. There, in the middle of the path was a large and breathtaking tree with berry-like clusters of fruit hanging in abundance. The clusters were very much like thin clusters of grapes. Yet, the fruit itself was similar to fresh gogi berries. They were small and very red. The tree grew so tall and wide that the top was not visible from where he stood.

Even more dazzling was the sight of the huge, intimidating creature standing next to the tree with its long neck wound through the branches. Its head moved slowly up and through, and then gracefully wound back down through the branches close to the couple standing under the tree. The creature had moved its head close to their faces the way it had done to David on the path. It was speaking in a strange language and the young woman was talking back to it.

David felt a pain rush through him as she reached to take a cluster of berries. The creature swung its head toward David staring at him with glistening eyes.

"NO!" David was screaming, realizing what he was about to witness. "NO!"

David turned to run. He felt like he was being chased and couldn't turn to look. He was still screaming, "NO!" as he ran. He didn't look back. He ran as hard as he could. He knew the couple could not see him. He was just a thought. He ran. He knew the creature *could* see him, even though he was just a thought. He couldn't think straight. His ability to run was failing. He tried to run harder. He felt like he was in a river of goo that was slowing his run. It was like many bad dreams he'd had where was trying to run from something and couldn't go fast enough!

Suddenly, with one last scream, "NO!" he felt, himself moving through something fluid and realized he was passing through the door of the vehicle that had brought him here. Once inside, he felt himself being pressed against the seat as it sped through space. He tried to sit correctly, but was having trouble doing so with the vacuum pushing him hard against the seat.

Finally, he was able to maneuver himself into a comfortable position. He felt a mixture of relief from his escape and sorrow at the loss of the garden and the voice he had communicated with. That voice that had filled every longing he had ever had was gone. That fellowship was lost. David wept. He wept for himself. He wept for the young couple, wondering how long they had actually lived there in communication with the voice. How long had they enjoyed the company and the fulfillment of communication and love with the one who created them with no more than a thought? How long had they been in fellowship with the one whose very hands had formed them carefully? Had they been there for days, or had they been there for decades, or even longer? David wept harder. "Now, their days are numbered." He whispered to the voice.

The voice did not answer. He could hear instead the sound of water. He tried to peer through the vehicle's fluid, translucent door but could see no source of the sound. Yes, it was definitely water gushing and bubbling. He closed his eyes in an effort to concentrate and hear which direction it came from. It seemed to be just outside the vehicle. He listened closely. Yes, it was water. And it was very close. He turned his head in the direction of the sound and slowly opened his eyes. He could see clearly through the translucent door. Everything had changed. Everything outside the vehicle was different.

Chapter 5

There were no lush gardens or giant trees. Instead, the ground looked dry and desert-like. He could still hear the water. As he stepped through the translucent vehicle to the outside, he saw where the sound was coming from. There was a large rock with water gushing out of it and bubbling all around it. The ground was so dry that David wondered why it was not absorbing the water instantly. Instead, the water was standing and forming a pool growing deeper by the second. He could hear heavy breathing; yet, he could see no one. He listened for several minutes. Then, he walked closer. He could hear the sound of breathing louder as he drew closer to the rock.

"Hello?" David spoke in a low voice, bracing himself so not to be startled by whoever must be hiding behind the rock.

"Hello."

"Hello?" David repeated.

There was no answer this time.

"Where are you? Who is it?" David stepped even closer and looked carefully behind the rock. He saw no one. He could still hear the sound of heavy breathing. David stuck his fingers in his ears and wiggled them trying to clear the passages to hear more clearly. He listened. The sound was still there.

David spoke again. "Hello?"

"Hello!"

"Who is it?" David continued to look all around walking around the rock. "Am I hearing things?"

"You are hearing me."

David stopped and looked at the rock. The voice was familiar. It was the voice of his young companion! David smiled and looked around, happy that he was not alone.

"Where are you?"

"I am …here!" David realized the sound came from the rock or the water, or both. He saw that the rock itself was moving slowly in and out as if it were breathing. The sound of breathing was coming from the rock! The voice rose out of the gushing water!

"Are you the…rock?" David felt very silly talking to a rock.

"I am!"

"Wow!" David moved to the rock to touch it and feel the gently heaving sides. He stuck his fingers under the water, and then cupped his hands to gather a drink. As he drank, he heard another sound.

Turning, he saw a strange man standing behind him. The man had a large walking stick in his hand and wore a long robe tied at the waist with a rope of braided leather. His skin was dark. His hair curled in dark ringlets with graying at the temples. He had heavy, dark brows and large, brown eyes etched with crow's feet. His lips were full and lined with deep laugh lines rising upward from his beard.

David swallowed the water in his mouth with a big gulp and stared at the man. "Hello!" The man did not move or look at David. He tried again. "Hello!" Still, the man did not respond.

David suddenly remembered that he could not be seen. "But, wait!" David turned, talking to the rock. He looked down and could see his own body. He had just dipped and swallowed water, but even as he thought it, he watched his form fade away.

The man was still staring at the water and the rock. David watched wishing he could be seen or heard. When the man finally turned to walk away again, David followed him. He walked slowly and steadily for a long distance. A haze shadowing the sun grew denser and the sky began to grow darker as they walked. Heavy clouds came over them and thick darkness fell suddenly.

David followed the sound of the footsteps ahead of him until the clouds moved and the sliver of a moon shed a small light. They grew close to a wall of rock. David had seen it in the distance earlier, but it seemed more looming and enormous as they came up to it. As the man began to climb the stony wall of rock, David stopped to watch. He waited for only a few seconds before following the man up the side of the rocky precipice. It didn't really take long to reach the top, verifying that David's original estimation was not off after all.

The man pulled himself up and stood on a flat rock at the top. Just below, David could barely make out the darkened form of tents and animals stirring. The man stood for a while. Then, he descended the other side and down into the camp of tents. Darkness fell in full force again as clouds hid the moon. David wondered that neither he nor the man fell or tripped down the jagged rocks. David followed him, moving closer as he made his way through the camp and into a tent. David sat down beside the man, who sat for several minutes, and then lied down with a heavy sigh. David wished the man could see him. He listened as the man's breathing slowed and grew deeper. A gentle, rhythmic snoring let David know he had dozed off into a sleep. He listened for several minutes. Then, he felt around and found the man's large walking stick. Slowly, he moved it away from the sleeping man. As he did, a glowing, rosy light grew inside the tent and David could see clearly. The stick was thick and heavy, yet David lifted it with ease.

A sharp light shot through the door of the tent. It landed on a shining object just at the man's side on his belt, which was still wrapped around his middle. David saw it was the metal of a large knife, unsheathed and stuck through the rope belt. He reached gingerly, pulling it out of its place very slowly. The man did not stir and continued to snore.

David ran his hand along the wooden staff carefully gliding his fingers over small lumps and natural grooves. He laid it across his lap as he sat cross-legged and held up the glinting knife as the sharp light shot against it again causing it to gleam as bright as a star. He turned the knife over a few times and checked it for sharpness. Touching the blade against the wood, he began to carve. He had planned to carve a walking stick for his aunt, who had specifically requested he do so. She had died before he had made her one. "This is for you, Aunt Petey." He barely whispered so not to awaken the snoring man, forgetting he could not be heard.

The night was long, but not long enough. David had barely carved his last line on the staff and returned it and the knife to their places when the man stirred and stretched. He sat back and watched as the man rolled to his side and reached to feel his staff, his eyes still closed. As he pulled it closer, his eyes opened and he lifted his head, looking at the staff. The man looked around as he sat up. He studied the details on the staff and ran his hand along it, looking around again. He stood and still looking around, he walked to the door of the tent and peered outside. He stepped back inside and studied the staff again. He closed his eyes, turned his face upward, and cried like a child for several minutes.

David stood and left the tent making his way to the rocky precipice. He began to climb. He reached the top, and then descended back down the other side. He wasn't sure what else to do. He wished he could talk with the man and tell him what he had done and why. He knew it would be futile. He could not be seen or heard. He felt loneliness flood through his soul. He rushed to get back to the rock, hoping to hear his young friend's voice again. He wanted to tell him about the staff and what he had carved. He knew that his companion would already know. He thought of the rosy glow in the tent and the sharp light glinting on the knife. Yes, He would know. He had been there with him. David was sure of it.

Stumbling here and there in the early morning's lingering low light, he ran, heading for the rock. It was nowhere to be found. David leaned his head back and shouted. "Hello!" There was no answer. He dropped to his knees in the sand and let his head fall, his chin almost touching his chest and feeling very lonely, yearning for something he could not name.

"I carved the staff," he said to no one, looking up. ""I am sure it was *the* staff. It was Moses, wasn't it?" He was questioning the sky. "I mean… the water and the rock, and a man with a staff. It had to be him. I carved it."

At that very moment, the man was still carefully observing the details carved in the staff. There was an elongated version of the rock with water coming from it on one side. Along the other side, there was the face of a child at the top, the face of an adolescent just beneath, the face of a man under that, and the face of the adolescent again. On the third side, there was a lamb, a cross, and small delicate rose petals. The man turned the staff and ran his fingers over the carvings. He turned to look at the tent door, and then bolted out of it with the staff in his hand. He ran past David, who felt him more than heard him. David rose and followed the man straight to the rock. When they got there, the man fell to his knees. He said with a bowed head. "Could water really come from a rock?" David was confused.

"Will water come from the rock?" David could see the water. The man was looking from the staff to the rock, and then back at the staff again.

Suddenly, the thought occurred to him that maybe he could see the water, but the man could not. After all, he couldn't be seen. Daylight began to rise on the distant horizon. The man was looking at the staff and caressing it worshipfully. He walked away from the rock and headed back to the camp.

David sat down by the rock and looked at it, listening to the music of the gushing water and gurgling bubbles till the sun shone hot and brightly in the sky. He could hear voices, many voices. He turned to see a crowd of people walking behind the man, heading straight for him. He hurried up to move out of their way realizing they would walk right through him, but accustomed by natural instinct to move and avoid being trampled.

The crowd stopped before reaching him and the man moved closer to the rock. David could hear whispers. He walked closer to the crowd to listen.

"Is he mad? There is no water out here! We will die before we find water!" David looked back at the rock in wonderment. They obviously could not see what he saw. A baby cried in the crowd and a child whispered someone's name.

David jerked around at the sound of a loud crack as the man struck the rock with the staff. The crowd was still for a second, and then the people began to shout, laugh, and dance, running into each other as they hurried to the rock cupping their hands to drink. The man stood holding the staff. He ran his hand along the carvings again. He watched as the people clamored for water. He turned away from the crowd, still caressing the staff.

The crowd stayed for the day, drinking and splashing in the water from the rock. When darkness began to fall, they turned to walk back to their camp. David watched as the man walked to the rock and took a last cupped handful of water and poured it over his head. He stared at the gushing rock. Then, he followed the crowd of people disappearing into the dusk of the evening.

David sat for a long while, and then decided to follow them. Darkness had closed them from his view. He began to run. He strained to see or hear something he could follow. The darkness grew thick and the stars gave no light as clouds grew over them.

Chapter 6

Twice, he tripped over sharp boulders in the path. He began to walk carefully trying to feel the path before each step. He could vaguely see a large object ahead of him. As he got closer, he reached out. He felt the side of the large wall of rock. He was sure if he moved slowly he could climb and find his way. Still straining to hear a sound, he made his way slowly and painfully up the side. One step at a time, he moved cautiously, not slipping at all. The night grew darker. The stars lit his way now and then when the clouds would break. He looked up to see if he could make out the top, but there seemed to be no end in sight. He continued to move upward. His arms grew tired and his legs were shaking. He was on the side of a cliff and he knew it was safer to keep going up than to try to go back down. Hours passed and he was still climbing.

Then, as he gripped to pull himself up again, he realized he could feel flatter ground. He pulled up and reached out to feel as far as he could. Either he was at the top or he had reached a jutting ledge he could pull himself up onto and rest a bit. He struggled with weakened arms to pull his full weight up and onto the ledge to a kneeling position. He felt around estimating that he had room to sit.

Several minutes passed. The clouds were hiding the stars and he sat waiting for them to reappear so he could get his bearings. He moved forward a few feet, and then to the sides feeling along the ground, crawling carefully. Yes, He must be at the top. Slowly and cautiously, he stood. He scooted his foot along to feel his way around and took a step or two.

A bolt of lightning lit up the entire night sky. The sound of thunder crashed and rumbled. David sat back down. He had been looking up when the lightening cracked. He would wait for another bolt of lightning to see his way. None came. Minutes passed. A sudden downpour of rain hit him like a bucket of water. He had no idea where he could find shelter.

He waited, hoping for lightening to light his way. He began to shiver and he saw his body was more visible. There was nothing he could do but sit in the pouring rain.

Finally, when he could no longer take it, he stood up and tried to feel his way along the top of the cliff. The rain was beginning to slow. He moved along gingerly wishing he could see. A thick fog was moving in around him and he wanted to get to some sort of shelter before he was entirely drenched. He took a step and slipped, losing his footing and falling forward. To his horror, he did not hit the ground! He continued to fall.

He knew he was falling off the edge of the other side and had no idea how far it was to the bottom. He hit his head on the side of a jutting rock and pain bolted through it. He felt himself losing consciousness and closed his eyes hoping to drift off, realizing that unconsciousness might save him from the pain and panic of his impending death, which was a certainty now.

David awakened with a start. It was lighter, the clouds having disappeared. He had not expected to awaken this time. To his surprise, he was still in a free fall. Thoughts began to race. Had he awakened just in time to feel the impact of death? He forced himself to look. He could not see the ground below. He was moving fast. There were walls of rock all around him. It was dark below and there seemed to be no bottom. That thought sent sheer terror through him "The bottomless pit?" He cried out. Had he already died? Was he heading in hell's direction? Terror raced through him like lightning bolts stinging his fingertips and toes.

"Oh, God!" He shouted. "Oh, God, oh God, oh, God! I am going to hell! Oh, God!" He was crying and falling. "No-o-o! I'm sorry. Please!" He looked below at the darkness. Once again, he was filled with surprise as he began to see that beneath him there was water, not fire, but water! Hope surged through him. "Please, not hell. Please!"

As he fell fast toward the water, he started to cry out one more time. He hit the surface of the water cutting through it like a knife. Pain shot through his stomach and legs. He sunk for several yards. As his body began to slow, he started swimming upward in strong strokes. The water was cold and dark. He couldn't make out the surface for sure, but thought he saw light and swam in its direction. His arms were tiring as he finally surfaced. His lungs ached as he sucked in air coming up out of the water. The sky was far away and stars were so distant they gave little light. The walls of the canyon he had fallen through were not visible. He could see small amounts of starlight here and there on the surface of the water; but, for the most part, all was dark and cold around him. Even in the cold and unfamiliarity of darkness, David felt relief. He was sure this could not be hell. Water and cold were far from what he could envision of what he supposed hell to be.

But, where was he? Where had he fallen to? In the distant sky, he heard the screech of a prey bird and the call of an owl. He heard the howl of a wolf, and then several more. Their lonely calls sent chills down his already cold spine.

David wanted to swim to move and get his body warm. He wasn't sure if he should. He was unsure of which way to go. The relief of not being in hell quickly faded, replaced by panic and desperation. He felt something rub against his legs. Whatever it was, it was immense. Panic raced through him again! He was sure it must be a shark! A wave rose and lifted him just above the large creature. He could feel it brush his feet.

"Oh, God!" He whispered this time, trying not to move. He held as still as the rolling water would allow. He felt the body of the creature move along under him.

David remembered the huge creature he had seen the children ride. It must be every bit as big as that creature. Then, just as suddenly, there was nothing, only the rolling and cold, dark water. He had to move enough to keep his head above the surface, but he did so timidly. "Oh, God," he whispered again. The water stirred and sent him bobbing to the right. A strange sound like a vacuum filled the air and a smell that almost made him vomit came bellowing at him in a rush of wind. The water was moving him fast; and suddenly, all was quiet. It was deathly quiet!

David could feel the movement of the water subside. He could touch the bottom. Seaweed and debris was floating and swirling all around him tangling his arms and legs, causing him to have difficulty moving. The stench was so nauseating, he had to vomit. He heaved until his stomach hurt. He tried to maneuver around and feel as he walked, trying to be careful not to step in any sudden deep holes. The dark was riveting! The stars had completely disappeared. He could see nothing.

Suddenly, a wall of water came rushing over him, knocking him down, rolling and tumbling him, and wrapping him even tighter in the tangle of seaweed. He was under water for only a few seconds when the water subsided. He tried to unwrap from the seaweed enough to stand. He vomited again. He wasn't sure if the smell or the rolling had caused him to vomit. He vomited seawater, not having realized he had swallowed it until then.

He was unsteady. The ground was moving under him. He was sure that he must be experiencing an earthquake and maybe a tsunami. Water rushed over him again, rolling and thrashing him around. He was dizzy and sick. The water subsided again. He tried to walk on the unsteady surface. He thought he heard someone call out. His ears were filled with water and seaweed wrapped his head.

Then again, a voice in the darkness called out. "In Trouble! I am in deep, deep trouble. I prayed to God from the belly of the grave. I cried for help." The voice was weak and trembling. "You heard my cry."

"Yes, I did!" David was trying to find the direction from which the voice came.

"You threw me into the depth of the ocean! I am in a grave of water."

"Hello! Where are you? I didn't throw you here! I am stuck here, too. Where are you?"

"The ocean waves and the tides are crashing over me."

"I know! Me, too! Where are you?"

"Oh, I cried out. I have been thrown away from your sight!"

"I am trying. I can't see you. Can you see me?"

"I will never lay eyes on the holy temple again."

David tried to hear the direction of the voice, now growing clearer.

"I think I am closer. Can you see me?"

"The ocean has me gripped by the throat. The abyss has grabbed me and held me tight."

"I am all tangled, too." David was trying to pull off the seaweed.

"My head was all tangled in seaweed at the bottom of the sea where mountains take root."

"Yeah, it smells gross, too!" David knew he was getting closer.

"I was as far down as a body can go and gates were slamming shut behind me forever."

"I know. I fell a long way. Did you fall, too?"

"You pulled me up from that grave alive, O God, my God."

"Wait, I'm not God…"

"My life was slipping away and I remembered God and my prayer got through to you."

"Oh. I thought you thought I was God. I still can't see you."

"My prayer made it all the way to the holy temple. Those who worship hollow gods walk away from their true love. But I am worshipping you, God. I am calling out in thanksgiving!'

"Wait…I am not God. I am … Can you hear me?"

"I will do what I promised I'd do! Salvation belongs to God!"

At that moment a wave crashed over David throwing him and tumbling him away from the voice. The water stopped moving. David was thrashing, still covered with water and tangled in seaweed.

Suddenly, the water carried him with force, shooting him through space and air. He could see the stars above at a great distance. He fell with a thud on hard land. His ribs hurt. He was coughing up seawater. He was cold and tangled in seaweed.

David heard weeping. "Hello?" There was no answer. He could hear the man. He could make out the sky and the water's edge. He could see the form of a man, tangled in seaweed just like he was. He was kneeling, bent over, and weeping on the beach just a few feet away.

"Hello?" David moved closer. "Hello?"

It was obvious the man could not see or hear him even though his body seemed to be more visible. The sky was growing light. He heard a loud sound and turned to see a fish leap in the air and come splashing down into the water. It was every bit as big as a whale, but seemed to be more streamlined, a giant creature. A huge wave slapped on the beach. David felt faint. His stomach still hurt from vomiting. The thought caused his stomach to lurch again. He spit out pieces of seaweed. His lips were salty and sore. He pulled off the remaining strands of seaweed and lie down holding his sickened stomach. He wiped his eyes with the other arm, and then closed them. As the sun rose over him, he slept.

David awakened. He felt himself being lifted and floating in the air. He felt as light as a feather. He could feel himself rising. Slowly, with his body still flat in a prone position, he began to rise in slow motion in a circular rotation higher and higher. David looked up into the darkening sky. The moon was crescent and bright. Stars were beginning to show up, twinkling white against the indigo sky. It was a clear and beautiful night. He could see one star in particular shining brighter and brighter. It seemed to grow bigger or closer. David wasn't sure which. Suddenly, the star seemed to shoot straight at him. He felt himself being lifted faster, and then pulled right into the center of the bright star.

The light was intense, but broken, as if it came from several sources. Giant diamond-like structures were exploding all around him as he traveled into the white light of the star. He could feel the star lifting and carrying him away. His body was limp like a rag. Yes, his body was back! He could see it! His arms were helplessly flapping and his legs were flailing around. He was being sucked as if by an enormous vacuum. He had no control over the force of it or what it was doing to his limbs.

As suddenly as he had been whisked away, the motion stopped and he found himself suspended inside an orb of some sort. The huge diamonds continued to explode around him. They appeared, exploded, and then appeared again. He moved his arms and wiggled his legs suspended in mid-air in the center of the orb. Gem-like colors were glowing, fading, and then glowing again all around him, lighted by the explosions of light.

He looked around. He could see only light and colors above and all around him. But, when he looked down, he could see straight through the orb of light to the earth below. The orb was moving toward the earth in slow-motion.

Closer and closer, it came until David could make out mountains, oceans, and land. The orb was slowing and moving along horizontally even as it grew closer. Below, he saw small outlines of what first appeared to be a trail of ants; and then, he saw it was a caravan of camels, donkeys, and many people. The orb continued to move horizontally as the caravan moved along in the same direction. It moved out in front of them, leading the way.

The light was intensifying and colors were becoming brighter and brighter. The orb moved along with David suspended in its center for days. At times, he would close his eyes and sleep, awakening excited to discover he was still suspended in the orb. After several days, David became restless. He felt anxious and an anticipation of some looming event began to stir inside him. He watched the caravan below; and suddenly, the orb swooped away from them in one swift motion carrying David up and away.

Music began to vibrate throughout the orb and the diamond-like structures began to explode and appear faster and faster. The music grew louder and louder. Suddenly, the orb stopped still. The music became clear and distinct. David could hear voices singing. He looked below and could only see darkness. The light inside the orb grew whiter and brighter and began to shoot out into the atmosphere lighting the darkness below.

David could see clearly now. He drew in a sharp breath when he realized where he was. He should have known! Nestled below him was a small town. It was an ancient village, reminding David of many Christmas cards he had seen. He knew exactly where he was! He strained to see what he knew to be below him at this very moment. He could not see that far. He could feel it though.

The sound of gushing water reverberated through the orb. "I am..." David could hear it in the center of the orb. "I am…" David felt reverence overwhelm him. He wanted to fall on his face but remained suspended in mid-air. Everything in his entire being needed to fall prostrate and he could not! He knew what was below him. He shouted, "The City of David!"

At the same time, he heard the sound of water rushing louder. "I am…" and then, he heard a cry. It was tiny and distant, but he heard it. The sound of the water stopped. The diamonds stopped exploding. The colors were fading and David could feel himself begin to fall. He was falling faster and faster toward the earth.

Strangely, David felt no fear this time. There was an acceptance of fate that flooded him with peace. He fell through the air. He could feel the wind rush and ripple through his clothes. He held out his arms feeling the force of his fall, closed his eyes, and lost consciousness.

Awakening, David looked around. He was again in the vehicle. He was able to see through its fluid walls. He was traveling through space. He could see the earth in the distance as he traveled toward it. All around him were colors, visible gasses, clouds, and sparkling floaters. They painted scenes in the empty space outside. He could see purple forms in the distance, beyond the blue planet growing closer. The purple forms seemed to have large blue clouded wings. He could see light piercing through them like a lightning bolt. There were more of the gases swirling in tornado forms off to his right. They faded into the space around them.

To his left, he saw distant stars in dark space. He saw fading and reappearing forms of colored clouds. It was like an enormous abstract painting, but living and moving, continually being painted, erased, and then painted again in different colors.

Suddenly, he could see himself on the outside of the vehicle floating in space. He was startled. "Me," he thought aloud. He could see himself as a toddler. He must have been about 3 or

4 years old. His hair was blonde and cut like a bowl on his head. He was hiding something behind his back, crying and throwing a tantrum. Tears were staining his dimpled cheeks. His expression was angry and strained. Next to him sat a toddler about the same age.

The little boy's dark locks hung in curls around his small brown face, framing huge amber eyes that slanted upward. The little boy's face was round with healthy, glowing cheeks. A smile of joy caused the boy's eyes to twinkle as he fondled a small box, turning it over and over in delight. It was delicately carved. The little boy giggled, shook the small box in toddler fashion, and held it out toward the vehicle as if trying to hand it to David to share. David rubbed his eyes expecting the scene to fade into the dark space. It didn't.

The vehicle moved past the baby boys and David could see himself again. This time, he was a little older. He saw himself running through a parking lot, and then jumping into the trunk of a car to hide from his mother. He remembered. His mother had taken him to church and he had decided he did not want to go in. He saw his mother looking anxiously around. She looked sad and scared at the same time. He swallowed hard, realizing he had made her sad that day. He had not seen that look the day he had hidden from her. She looked around desperately holding back her tears.

As the vehicle sped past the scene, David saw another woman looking anxiously around.

Suddenly, she ran embracing a young boy sitting among several men with an ancient-looking scroll in his hand. The young boy stood and held his mother, whispering something as if to comfort her.

David began to weep again. Scene after scene past by him as he saw himself at different ages only to be contrasted by another boy the same age doing exactly the opposite of what David had done.

Scenes began flashing faster and faster. He saw himself as a young man laughing with other young men reaching for drugs; and then, he saw a young man turning his head from stones being offered in a desert. He saw himself in a fistfight; and then, he saw a young man reaching out to touch a man who had sores all over his body and deformed face with such a touch of tenderness that David wept even harder.

He saw himself responding to a young girl. He saw a young man standing on the top of a high mountain looking through space at the earth, and then turning to walk away.

He saw himself turning a bottle of alcohol up in a long drink, laughing in drunken stupor, and then a young man handing a cup of wine and a piece of bread to men sitting with him in sober sadness.

As the realization of his own ways sunk through him, piercing his very heart, he felt a jolt and blacked out in unconsciousness.

Chapter 7

David felt himself awaking from unconsciousness. He could smell dust and breathed it into his nostrils causing him to cough and choke. “Oh no! The lane!” He thought to himself. “I am waking up from a dream. This has been a dream!”

Pain suddenly seared through his body wracking every bone, muscle, and organ! He felt a weight on his back pressing him into the dust. His head was held down and he couldn’t lift or turn it. He could taste blood in his mouth. He could smell sweat, blood, and a stench he couldn’t quite place that caused his stomach to lurch, and he had to vomit. Vomit came up in his mouth and mixed with the taste of blood. He couldn’t lift his pounding head to turn it. His body was stinging. No, it was worse than that! He was in so much pain he felt as if he were going to go unconscious again.

Stinging, burning pain competed with the throbbing pulse and the heat surging through his body and across his skin. He could not bear the pain! He couldn’t breathe! The weight was too heavy! Panic was striking him at the very core of his being! He could hear a roar in his ears mixing with the sound of the blood pounding in them.

He tried to open his eyes but they were stuck shut and hurt in excruciating agony. He strained to make out the roar and realized it was voices screaming and laughing in a huge roar. “Kill Him!”

"Get up, David!" The words were jeering and mean. The roar was deafening. The throbbing in his head and the nausea overwhelmed him and he vomited again in his mouth choking on the blood, vomit, and dust as he breathed them into his lungs.

Something hit him hard in the ribs like a sharp kick. The crowd roared. He heard a whisper in strange language breathing into his ear with the smell of a horrid stench. He began to go unconscious from choking and lack of oxygen.

Suddenly, the weight lifted! David raised his head spewing out vomit and blood, choking, and breathing in air. The pain was gone. The taste of blood was gone. His head was not throbbing. He could still smell the dust and hear the crowd. He opened his eyes and turned his head to look into the swollen and bloodshot eyes of a badly bruised, swollen, and bloody man lying in the dust next to him. The eyes were the same slanted amber eyes of the child he had had seen in space, the same eyes of the youth, and the young man in the scenes so vividly contrasted with David's life.

A cross of rough wood was being lifted off of the man. With obvious effort, the man whispered, "I'll do it for you." Then crying out in pain as a blow from a sandaled foot shot into his ribs, the man spit out blood and vomit and his face fell into the dirt. Two men lifted the man to his feet.

David felt hollow. He felt empty. He felt that he was as void as anyone or anything could possibly be and still be alive. He looked down and saw his body was translucent again. As the man turned his swollen and bloody face to David, he spoke through blood-caked lips. The voice said, "That's right. Even now you are on my mind. You are what I am thinking about. You are as real as my thoughts."

The man doubled in pain as a heavy blow struck his stomach. Weakened from nausea and loss of blood, the man's body swayed and he dropped to his knees and hands. David reached to help him. His hand passed through the man's body.

"I can't help you!" It was a scream mixed with an agonizing sob. David shouted at the crowds in horror and realization, "He hasn't done anything wrong!" There was no response. The crowd could not see or hear him.

David swung around screaming at the crowd. "Let him go! He didn't do anything wrong! He took my place!" The crowd was getting louder. Some were spitting on the weakened man as he rose slowly to his feet reeling from pain. David threw his head back. With arms outstretched and clenched fists, he let out a bellow of sorrow. "NO!" The sound of his voice was overshadowed by the crazed crowd screaming and spitting, cursing and laughing. The man was slowly taking step after step hardly able to stand upright.

After a step or two, he looked back at David. His face was so swollen and bruised! It was so caked with blood and dirt that the bloodshot eyes could barely squint open. They stared deeply into David's soul. David dropped to his knees, held his face in his hands, and cried.

Flashes of the scenes he had just witnessed of his own life flooded his mind. "No," he whispered weakly. As the crowd surrounded the man and distance grew between them, David fell face first into the dust and again lost consciousness.

He woke up with a sigh that started deep in his spirit and rattled through his entire being. Once again, he awakened in the vehicle hurling through space. He closed his eyes and tried not to think. He didn't want to think or feel just then. All he had witnessed had been too huge to take in.

Of course, he had often thought about and read about the original sin. That sin had brought death to a beautiful existence originally designed for man. It was real to David now in a way it had never been before. He had been there! He had seen the beautiful garden. He had breathed in the existence of paradise on earth. He had felt and lived in the innocent experience of man existing and communing with his creator on a personal level. He had experienced walking and talking with God in the cool of the evening. He had felt the deep love and the yearning for the voice that came each night with the rising of the mist. He had hurt with the pain of longing for it when it was gone. The whole story had new meaning for him. He had lived it.

The vision of the fruit, the young woman, and the glistening, beautiful beast in the tree flashed through his thoughts. He remembered the look of the gleaming, knowing eyes of the beast. He could see in his mind that serpent-like creature glaring at him standing there as he witnessed the devastation of man on earth.

He had heard, and knew well, the story of the crucifixion. He had been very familiar with the fact that the crucifixion was an act of love, God taking his place and suffering what he deserved to suffer. Still, he had never *really* understood that *his* place was taken at that moment. He had never *really* thought about that place actually being lived out by him. Jesus had done it. It had never been something he would have to experience. It had always seemed more as if it were something he deserved because he was God's child and the crucifixion was somehow Jesus' destiny. Right now, David understood. It wasn't Jesus' destiny. It was *his* destiny. That torture and death was his to experience! That innocent child he had seen, the one so unlike him, had taken the place that David himself was destined to experience. He had done it for him.

David could remember the taste of blood and vomit mixed with dust. He remembered the pounding of his head, the pain, and the inability to lift his head or body. He remembered the heat and dizziness. He remembered the sound of jeering crowds and the shock of the blow in his aching side. Even the memory sent chills that seared like coals through his spirit. He would have vomited if he'd had a body to do it, but he didn't. He was only a thought. Yet, he yearned for the ability to rid himself of the foulness turning deep inside his spirit.

Again, he whispered to the voice, "Oh…Oh!" It was more like a breath than actual words. He felt sorrow deeper than any he had ever felt. It was burning and churning like a volcano wishing to erupt.

He groaned again, uttering from deep inside, "Ugh!" It was just a sound. He had no words that could express how he felt. He hoped the voice would hear it and come. He tried again to shut out his thoughts. As he desperately attempted to empty his mind, he felt the vehicle lurch to a stop that threw him forward into the dash and buttons.

In response, he threw his arms in front of him to stop the blow. He saw them pass through the dash with his face flowing closely behind. He was glad he was just a thought as his body passed through the vehicle's instruments, then shot backward completely through the seat, and then forward again.

Chapter 8

David sat still for a few seconds trying to clear his thoughts. He let out a sound of relief and sorrow mixed. He exited through the door of the vehicle, not waiting for it to open. As he moved through it, he lost his balance and fell face forward into a pile of sand. He could feel the heat of the sand and could smell the dust that engulfed his face. He lifted his head up, looking around. Waves of heat hovered above the sand. There were no trees or grass, only sand and one big rock. The sky was blue and cloudless, but too bright to look at. He rubbed his eyes and looked down, wondering if his body had returned. He could feel the heat. His body was there again. "I'm not a thought anymore," he said out loud to the rock.

"You are still a thought." It was the voice!

"You're here!" David's voice showed his joy.

"I am!"

"I have a body." David said to the voice.

"So do I."

David looked around! 'Where are you?"

"I am… right here."

"I can't see you." David looked down. "I can see me."

"I am here!" The voice had changed. David saw a child peek from behind the big rock. The child moved forward with a smile. “Were you looking for me?’

“I am not sure.” David was answering truthfully. He wasn’t sure who this child was. “I was looking for someone. I heard a voice and thought it was who I was looking for.”

“Who were you looking for?” The child smiled, tossing black curls out of his dark, olive-colored eyes. “You were talking to the rock.”

David had no answer to that.

“Were you looking for the rock?” Again, the child smiled, tossing the curls. He sat down crossing his legs. He had a straw in his hand which he stuck in his mouth and chewed on as he looked at David. David felt he had seen this child before, but he couldn’t quite remember where.

After a few seconds, the child spoke again. “You were talking to the rock.”

“I was talking to myself.” He realized it sounded rather defensive.

The child pursed his lips with the straw still between them, gave two nods as if in thought, and then said, “Would’ve been smarter to talk to the rock.”

With that, he got up with a chuckle and began to walk away.

David jumped up. “Where am I?” He was feeling stupider by the second.

“Right here. Where else would you be?”

“Well, where is right here?” He felt better. At least that question sounded sane.

The child stopped and looked back as if he had suddenly realized something.

“Come, I will show you. Follow me.” With that, the child turned and sprinted off.

David had some difficulty responding as quickly. He was still reeling a bit from the experiences he had just been through. He tried to keep up with the sandal-footed child.

He felt slow and inhibited as if running in a dream again. For just a moment, the memory of feeling energized and alive in the Garden flashed though his thoughts. The heat of the sand was burning his feet. He looked down realizing he was barefoot. He wished to be back in the place where he had been able to defy gravity and run just above the ground. He stopped to sit and lift his burning feet off the sand which caused him to lose track of the child. When he looked up, the boy was nowhere in sight. He strained to look farther, but the desert heat created waves of illusionary sights disappearing as quickly as they appeared. Wisps of movement crossed through the waves. He thought he saw the child. Then, the illusion disappeared. Again, he thought he saw him in the distance.

The heat was searing through the seat of his jeans. He timidly got up and tried to walk again.

The sand was too hot, so he decided to run hoping the swift movement might ease the sting of the sand. It didn't. Still, he ran faster. What else could he do? He was looking down at his burning feet as he ran when suddenly, with a painful thud, his run came to a short stop.

"UGH!" David rolled around on the hot sand holding his stomach. He had been so focused on looking down that he had not seen the huge rock in the way and had ran right into it, knocking the very breath from him. His lungs were stretching in a painful attempt to suck in air again.

"Oh! Ow!" he muttered once he had drawn in enough air to speak. He closed his eyes for just a second. When he opened them, he saw the boy standing over him with a slight smile and a twinkle in his dark eyes. He was still chewing on the straw. He didn't say a word. He pursed his lips, held the straw between his teeth, and shook his head. He shrugged his shoulders and turned to walk away. Looking back over his shoulder, he said, "Follow me. I'll walk."

David felt he had no defense left in him. He was utterly tired. His stomach hurt from the jar of running into the rock. He felt like vomiting again. His head was beginning to ache from the sun. His eyes were stinging and tired. He picked himself up and humbly followed the little child. In the distance, he could see a small tree. Hoping to relieve his feet in its shade, he hurried ahead. It was a small tree, but David was very grateful for it. The boy was close behind him. He sauntered up to join him in the shade.

As soon as he sat down, the boy ripped a piece of material from the hem of his robe-like garment and reached to take one of David's badly burned feet. Carefully, he wrapped the foot with the cloth. He repeated it again for the other foot. Neither spoke at all. When he was finished, the boy smiled, leaned back against the tree, and closed his eyes. He was still chewing on the straw.

"Thanks," David said, feeling more like a child than this little boy. The child's dark eyes flickered open. He nodded in affirmation and closed his eyes again. David leaned against the tree himself. He looked up through the branches. Sitting on a limb about two thirds of the way to the top was a beautiful eagle. It was watching David. As he sat up to get a better view, the bird took wing and rose to the sky. It soared and dropped, then rose again calling to the two under the tree in long, echoing cries. It circled high on the waves of the wind. He wondered how it could find waves to ride on in so still a sky.

"Ever wish you could fly?" It was the first thing the boy had said in a while. He was staring at the graceful bird of prey.

"Yeah," David answered. He wiped the sweat from his brow, wishing for water.

"Here," the boy was handing him a canteen made of wrinkled leather-looking material. For once, David did not think about who had been drinking from it. He took a gulp of the water. It was hot, but still soothed his lips and throat.

"It is really hot here. Thanks for the shoes." David looked down at his wrapped feet and the torn hem of the boy's clothes. "Thanks." Again, the boy pursed his lips and gave a quick, affirming nod.

"Ready to go?" asked the boy.

"Sure."

"Watch out for rocks." It was a mumbled sentence. David felt no offense this time. He smiled to himself. Even though his feet felt dry and hot, the wrapping definitely improved the walking.

The eagle continued to soar above them calling to them in a distant cry. David and the boy looked up every now and then. Both of them were imagining how it must feel to fly, but neither spoke for a while.

"Where we going?" asked David.

"Right there," replied the boy with a point of his finger. David could see a wavy outline in the heated distance. As they walked closer and closer, it began to take form. There was a makeshift shack. Beyond that, there was a huge tent. David could hear the sound of animals mingled with the eagle's cries. As they grew closer, he could see small kid goats and lambs. They were crowding around another young man. David estimated him to be in his late teens or early twenties.

"David!" the young man's voice was stern. "Where have you been? Who is this?"

The young man was looking at him as if he was an alien. He looked at David's face, and then at his clothes. David returned the gesture. His skin was bronze from the sun. His bearded face and wrapped head indicated that David was in the presence of foreigners. Yet, they were speaking to him in his language! They called him by name!

"I …" David and the boy answered and stopped in unison, turning to look at each other. Then, again in unison, "I was…" They smiled at each other and tried again.

"I'm David," they both said at once to each other. This time they laughed. David reached out his hand for a handshake. "I am David."

The older youth looked at David's hand, and then at the boy. "What are you up to, Brother?" His voice was suspicious and agitated. "Who is this…," he looked David up and down, stopping to stare at the wrapped feet. "Person," he finished.

David and the boy both started laughing. This only agitated the boy's older brother further. David could not help it. He had been through so much, the release of laughter overtook him and he held his already hurting stomach.

"I found him talking to the rock," the boy could hardly say it in his mirth. The two Davids laughed even harder. David's eyes were stinging with tears of laughter and his stomach was aching more.

The older youth shook his head and walked off. David realized where the boy had learned that behavior.

"He can't help it, Brother," said the child catching up to his brother. "He just keeps bumping into rocks!" He was trying to sound serious and was looking back at David, who started the laughter between them all over again.

"Father!" The older youth was yelling. "Father! David has brought a madman here!" He looked down on his little brother with a look of authority that stopped the child in his tracks and ended the laughter.

An older man came out of the tent, pushing back the flap. He eyed the child with agitation.

"The lambs came home without you!" He had ignored the fact that David was standing there except to look at him up and down.

"I'm sorry, Father. There was a lion." The boy was looking down at his torn hem.

The Father looked at the garment, then at David's feet.

"A lion? David, when did you start telling such stories?"

"Father," the boy looked up, "there was a lion! The lambs ran off when I was killing him."

The old man looked at David's feet.

"Did the lion rip your clothes and then give the cloth to the madman?" David wanted to defend himself. He started to step forward to say he wasn't mad when he saw the look of mirth cross the old man's lips and the twinkle in his eye. Again, David recognized where the boy had learned his behaviors and his wit.

The old man tussled the boy's curls; and then, he said sternly, "You will stay with me tomorrow!" The boy started to argue, but stopped before a word was uttered when he saw the stern look his father gave him.

"You will stay with me until you learn to be responsible for what is in your care!"

David looked at the boy and saw a tear form and run down his dusty, tanned face. The boy looked at David. David stepped forward.

"Excuse me, Sir," he said to the old man. "Your son helped me..."

The old man held up his hand to say stop. David stopped and looked at the boy, who shrugged and walked off to the tent with shoulders slumping.

"Are you hungry, my friend?" The old man swept his arm in a welcoming motion toward the tent. David followed the motion, stepping inside the tent as the old man stood to the side. The boy sat cross-legged on a rug, looking like a scolded puppy.

"Sit," the old man motioned for David to sit. He purposely sat across from the boy so he could catch his eye and hopefully apologize with a look for his inability to help. The child kept his eyes down.

The old man sat and crossed his legs. The older youth came into the tent with a glance at his younger brother. Another young man entered and sat. Two others soon followed. A woman entered carrying a large pot. She sat it on a rug of animal hide in the center of the circle of men.

Two young girls brought in loaves of bread. Another young woman came with containers that she filled with the brew from the pot which she passed one by one to the men, starting with the old man and ending with the boy. She looked at David, and then at the old man. He nodded. She brought David a container.

The old man raised his container and the rest all did likewise as he prayed a blessing. A loaf of bread was passed around. Each one tore off a piece and dipped the bread in the brew. David followed suit.

He ate his food quickly. It seemed like years since he had eaten anything at all. Dinner was eaten in silence. The meal was followed by conversation.

"So, David," both Davids looked at the old man. He was looking at the boy. "Who is your friend?" The child looked for confirmation from David as he spoke.

"This is David…also." David nodded. "I found him talking to the rock."

At this, the old man turned to study David. Then, without taking his eyes off David, he asked the boy, "And what was he saying to the rock?"

"He said, 'I have a body.'"

"And, what did the rock say to that?" The old man was looking at David.

David spoke carefully, "It said, 'so do I.'" Everyone except the old man laughed. David kept his eyes focused on the old man since he was the only one not laughing. "It said I was still a thought. It said, 'I am here'. I know that sounds crazy. Maybe it was the crash or the heat. I was sure I heard it! It was the voice I talked to in the Garden!"

The old man stood suddenly and with a distinctive wave, everyone became quiet and left the tent with surprise on their faces. The child looked back at David concerned, stopping for a brief second as he passed through the tent opening.

The man stayed standing. "Who are you?" The question seemed anxious, almost fearful.

"I'm David, Sir."

"Where are you from and why are you here?" It was asked respectfully.

"Well, I am from a different time, I think. From the way you are dressed, I think this may be a time before I was born. I guess it might just be my time and I am in a different country than my own. I am not really sure. I have been on a strange journey, Sir. I have seen the future. I have seen the Garden. I have witnessed the death of…" David stopped. "Is your son David, the King?"

Up to that point, the old man seemed to be unsurprised at David's story. With the last question, he simply left the tent. David could hear muffled conversation outside the tent. The old man was talking to someone.

"Father?" It was the child.

"Your friend is a madman!" The old man's voice was strained and he spoke as if speaking to himself. "What kind of story did you tell him, my son?"

David was peering out the opening of the tent. He saw the old man, who was walking back to the tent stop short, and then lean to look into the boy's eyes.

"Why are you so suddenly telling stories? What did you tell this man? That you are a king? A king who kills lions by himself?" The old man's hands were waving in the air. His face looked anxious. The mirth was missing. "What am I to do with you? I have changed my mind. You shall watch the flock tomorrow! Should you meet any more lions..." With a wave of his hand, he walked to the tent.

"Father!" The boy's voice caused his father to stop and turn to him. "I have something for you!" With that, David watched the boy reach in a pouch strapped over his shoulder. "Here," he said bowing slightly and putting something in his father's hand. As he bowed, he looked at David with a slight smile, and then he ran off.

The old man looked in his hand and drew in a quick breath, looking back up at the boy. He looked in his hand again and stood there as if paralyzed staring at whatever gift his son had given him.

David slunk back into the tent and sat back in his place wondering what had just happened. The old man finally reentered the tent and sat, still staring in his hand. David sat quietly. Finally, the old man spoke, "Did you see him do it? Did you see the lion?"

David looked at the old man with a question in his eyes, unsure of what to say. The old man reached across the rug offering the gift in his hand to David. When he dropped it into his open hand, David looked instantly back at the old man. It was a large fang of an animal tied onto a piece of thread with a tuft of golden animal hair.

David felt very tired. He felt overwhelmed. So much was happening so fast that he couldn't seem to take it all in.

The old man was speaking, "Did the rock tell you anything else…." David slipped into a faint with no answer. The heat, the stress, the experiences, and the emotions he had recently experienced whirled through his conscience and faded off with the words.

David slept late into the evening. A strange, beautiful sound whispered into his dreams and David's eyes opened to see the young boy sitting at the door of the tent with his back to David. He was looking at the sky and singing in a voice that touched David's very soul and brought tears to his eyes. He wasn't sure if he had ever heard such a beautiful voice. The boy began to hum, and then turned as David sat up and stretched.

The child looked back at the sky and began singing a little clearer and louder. He was pretending not to have noticed David sitting up. The words were distinct.

> "Sleep, yes sleep, my friend, my friend who is so mad.
> He talks to stones and rocks, whenever he is sad!
> Hmmmm, hmmmm,
> He follows little kings, Hmmmm hmmmm,
> And wakens when one sings.
> He walks on heated feet and runs into big rocks.
> He follows baby kings who really watch the flocks. Hmmm, hmmmm.

"Very funny!" David stretched again and got up walking over to the boy. "So, are you King David from the Bible?"

"From the what?"

"Never mind."

"I'm not a king! You hit that rock too hard; or, your head is still full of the sun! I am the last son of Jesse. I am a shepherd when my father lets me. I am far from a king." He smiled, holding up his torn garment. "I may have passed for one before, but now I never will…" He shook his head in feigned sorrow. "Nope, I do not look like a king anymore! But you do! Look at your royal shoes." He giggled pointing at the pile of torn material that had been removed from David's feet before the meal.

"My father believes you. I can see that. He thinks you actually talked to the rock."

"I did! You heard me!" David was playing back now, intrigued by the quick wit and intelligence of the boy.

"Yes, but he believes the rock talked to you! My father is an old man."

"And, I am a madman! Guess we should get along good."

The boy nodded. He looked at the stars and began to sing.

"So, you really killed a lion," David had lied down on his back by the tent opening, looking up at the starry sky.

The child sang his answer.

"He came rushing at my flock and I began to shout.
I ran toward him fast and he just turned about.
He looked at my small hands and growled in ecstasy.
He raised his fangs to laugh. He imagined eating me.

His tongue began to lick his lips as if he
knew how good I'd taste.
I said a prayer so fast. I had no time to waste.
I sang a song of praise. The lion heard me
sing.
He saw a little boy, but his heart could hear a
king.
I ripped him with my hands as I sang out
loud.
When I had finished him, to the rock
bowed...."

The boy looked at David with a mischievous look, stood, and walked away.

Chapter 9

David sat for a while, thinking. He had spent so much time experiencing everything. He had not spent enough time analyzing it all. He pulled a piece of straw-like grass from a clump beside him and stuck it between his teeth to chew on as he pondered. He smiled. He was doing something he didn't usually do, but had seen his companions of late do. "Guess you really do become like those you hang around!"

He lied back on the sandy earth, chewed, and pondered. Hearing the familiar sound of a distant eagle, he strained to get a glimpse. He could only see a black spot. It was so high he wasn't sure if the sound came from it or not. He gazed at the horizon and searched the sky.

Looking around to be sure no one was watching or listening, he whispered. "Hello." He was hoping to hear the voice again. A cool breeze crossed his face and he heard a faint whisper.

"Wait."

David waited, unsure if he had really heard anything at all. After a few minutes, he tried again, "Hello?" Nothing happened. There was no answer. David closed his eyes to rest and the breeze blew across his face again. Another whisper reached his ears.

"Wait."

David was still. Even if he hadn't heard anything, it wouldn't hurt to just be still and wait. He waited. He listened to the sound of his own breathing and the distant cry of the eagle. The sound grew louder and closer. He kept his eyes closed, waiting. He wanted to call out again. He waited. The minutes passed. The day was growing hot, but David had fallen asleep lulled by the sound of his own rhythmic breath.

He woke with a start, his head hurting slightly. The sun was beating down so brightly he could barely open his eyes. He could feel the burning sun on his arms. Strangely, he couldn't really distinguish his arms. It felt like he had many arms. He tried to use them to sit up and couldn't quite get the feel of where they were. He stopped moving to get his bearings. Were his arms asleep?

No, in fact, he could feel them and move them. There just seemed to be a lot of them! He tried again to use his arms to sit up where he could see better and he felt a pull and a sharp pain. He looked down at his right side and saw that his elbow and forearm was pushing on what looked like a wing with huge feathers.

He tried to sit up again pushing against the wing. He could feel the pulling again and a slight shooting pain. Shocked, he shot up onto his feet! Breathlessly, David turned quickly to the right and to the left, and then in a complete circle attempting to look around his own body.

The wings were attached to him and he could feel them as if they were apart of him, like extra arms! He tried to move them and they moved. He had the same control over them as he did his arms, his hands, and his fingers! He could move the whole wing, or both, since there was one on each side. He could stretch them out and fold them up. He could move a tip or the whole side. He had wings!

He looked up at the sun and had to close his eyes quickly. This time, he was sure he must be dreaming. The heat had burned his brain. Maybe he was having a hallucination from heat stroke. He moved his arms, and then his wings. He moved them together. Yes, they were equally as controllable as both of his arms and his legs.

He felt the cool breeze again. Then, the breeze hit him with a force almost blowing him over. He heard the cry of the eagle again. He looked around seeing the tents and the shack. He could see movement, but no one coming his way. He searched the surroundings for the boy, or anyone. No one was there.

He closed his eyes and listened to the eagle. He felt the breeze again strongly, but not as forceful. He took in a purposefully deep breathe and began to run. He ran fast, and then, faster.

He could feel the breeze under his arms and he stretched out the wings, still running. A gust of wind lifted him, his feet still moving. He was barely off the ground as the breeze died out again. He tried several times to use the wings. A few times, the breeze lifted him slightly. He continued to run, trying to run harder.

After a while, he slowed his pace, rubbing his chin in thought. He turned, changing directions. This time he ran away from the dwellings instead of parallel to them. He ran at an angle to the wind.

When he could feel the pressure of running against the breeze, he unfolded his wings and was lifted a little higher and a little longer than before. He was flying. True, he was barely off the ground, but he was off the ground! He briefly thought of his burning feet the day before.

David watched the sky for the eagle. He could still hear it. Each time the breeze gently let him back to the ground, he kept his feet moving to gain lift again. He closed his eyes, enjoying the feel of the breeze lifting him on the wings as he glided just above the ground.

Suddenly, he felt the wind lift him and carry him upward. He smiled and then, "UGH!" The huge groan was knocked from him with his breath, and he felt himself dropping. He opened his eyes to see he had hit the side of a mountain. He looked down to see how far he was falling just as he hit the ground with a thud! At least, he hadn't fallen very far.

Still, he had hit hard and one wing was unfolded and hurting. He pulled himself out of the hot sand by holding onto the rocky wall. He stood half bent over to get his wind fully back, and then moved his wing to see if it still worked. It folded back. It seemed to be working. He stood up, brushing his arms to remove sand. He had a few scratches and his chest hurt from the impact. At least, he had been holding his head up and back feeling the wind and had not hit head first.

"I just flew." He spoke, not caring about the scratches or pain. He looked at the rocky side of the cliff. He found some jutting edges and began to climb. The weight of the wings did not seem to hinder his climb at all. He was careful to keep his footing and find solid gripping on each jutting edge. He really didn't want to fall and chance damaging his new appendages. He looked back once hoping the boy had followed him and could see what was happening.

So far, he had been experiencing everything alone. He wished for the company of the child. He missed the conversation and the witty exchanges. He turned back to the rocky wall remembering he had purposely decided to do this walkabout on his own. It was his own decision to isolate himself from people to get a better connection with God. It had been his choice. The recent friendly conversation with the child made him feel very lonely though. He wanted to hear the sound of another voice.

"Hello," he said again as he climbed. Trying again to hear the voice he had heard in the Garden, from the rock, and in the breeze earlier. No one answered him, but he felt a breeze blow lightly across his face and he tightened his grip on the jutting edges in case a larger gust might follow and blow him off the side. He could hear the call of the eagle in the distance. He began to hear the faint sound of water. He could barely make it out, but it was definitely water pouring and splashing onto water. It grew louder as he climbed.

He had to stop often to catch his breathe. He did his best to wipe the perspiration from his eyes by using his shoulder cautiously. He was very hot and his hands were beginning to feel slippery. Several times, he looked down, knowing it was too far to try to go back. Several times, he looked up, fearing he might slip before he reached the top. It took a good hour for David to reach the top of the rock wall. When he finally felt the top edge and pulled himself up, he took one last look down to gage the distance he had climbed.

The wind blew against him as he stood at the top. It was cooler and felt good against his wet body. The sun was shining brightly and he could feel its heat, but the air was not as hot. He stretched his arms, and then the wings, feeling the air slightly lift him. He stood that way for a while, getting the feel of the wind.

Then, as if by some invisible signal, he turned away from the cliff's edge and ran for several yards. He stopped. He turned back to face the edge of the cliff in anticipation. He stood for at least one minute. Then, he spoke, "Why not?"

With a loud and long shout, David ran at full speed toward the cliff's edge, and just before he reached the edge, spread his wings. With complete abandon, he ran off the edge. He felt himself drop! Fear sent icy stabbing pain through his body. The sudden drop forced all the air out of his lungs. He watched the ground growing closer. Forcibly sucking in air, he was able to fill them enough to let out a cry, "Help!"

Immediately, he felt the impact of lift as the wind lifted him, breaking his fall. He felt wind under and through his wings. It was moving along his body like water in a river. It carried him like waves of the ocean, and every now and then dropped and picked him up again. A gust of wind hit him from the side and changed his direction. Then, another turned him almost upside down. He began to feel the waves coming and used his wings to glide over them as he learned their direction and flow. He began to fly with ease, and finally, with complete control.

He began to shout and call back to the eagle. On a turn to the right, he saw the eagle gliding beside him. It cocked its head, peering at him with dark eyes. Then, it tilted its body soaring off and to the right like a fighter plane. He tried to imitate the move and began to roll and lose control for a few moments.

He struggled to right himself again. He looked behind at the mountain he had climbed growing smaller in the distance until it faded out of view. David continued to soar, unsure of how to turn and ride the waves in another direction.

He looked down wondering how he was going to ever touch the ground again without falling. It was getting easier to glide, but he wasn't sure where to go from there. He began to grow anxious. He realized he had just made another decision without thinking it through to the end. He should have planned how he was going to land before taking the leap.

Just as he began imagining possible results of his actions, he felt the wind waves grow weaker. Panic set in! “Concentrate!” He was shouting to himself. “Birds land. Planes land.” He was talking to himself. “You can do this!” David tried to feel the waves of air. He focused his mind. He could feel the direction of the wind. He closed his eyes and attempted to focus harder. “Yes,” he thought. He could feel one wave, and then another. He concentrated. With his eyes still closed, he began to dip and turn and follow different waves. He could feel the skin on his face rippling. Every now and then a large wave of air would lift him higher again. Then, the wave would drop him and he’d catch another wave that would turn him to the right or left.

He kept his eyes closed to be able to continue to focus and concentrate. He let out a long, high call trying to sound like an eagle. As the cry escaped his lips, he let it call long and as loud as the wind against his face would let him. David had never felt anything like this. It was pure ecstasy!

Taking in a huge breath to let another call escape, David felt his whole body ripple as he crossed what he was sure must have been turbulence. His whole body was bouncing against wind waves. He opened his eyes just in time to see himself plunge through the turquoise surface of a body of water.

David had not let out his breath to make the last cry. The force of the impact caused some of his breath to escape as his face and chest hit the surface. The speed at which he was travelling carried him forcefully through and to the depth of the water. He attempted to use his arms and legs to slow himself, fearing he was going to hit the bottom at any time.

He tried to stretch his wings now folded perpendicular to his body from the force of the dive. With all his might, he tried to pull them forward to slow his descent before he went any deeper. He continued to hold his breath. His lungs were aching.

He had gone so deep, he was sure he would never be able to hold his breath long enough to reach the top. The water was dark. He had slowed considerably. He attempted to bring his wings in again and was able to do so, bringing himself to a stop in the deep darkness. He immediately began to try to surface by using his arms and feet, as well as the immense wings, thinking they would allow him a faster exit from the deep waters.

Determination to stay alive crossed his face. He kept swimming as hard as he could. He felt the last of the air escape slowly from his tight lips as the bubbles passed his nose. He was sure he could determine himself to get to the top. The darkness remained. In fact, it seemed to be growing darker so he stopped. His lack of air caused a searing pain to pull at his lungs. He was confused. He was no longer sure which way was up or down.

His brain began to feel foggy and he closed his eyes, accepting the inevitable. He consciously focused his mind imagining the face of Jesus. He had drawn Him once. He imagined himself drawing that picture. His mother had told him that if he focused on Jesus completely he was guaranteed perfect peace. He had no choice but to try it right then.

Intense peace flooded his entire being. He focused on the face in the drawing in his mind and let his lungs try to suck in the air he knew they would not gain. As he breathed in, accepting his fate, he felt himself smile and relax. Air filled his lungs! He opened his eyes! He was still in water, but the water was no longer dark! It was a deep turquoise with a rose and golden glow. He was surrounded by the most unusual creatures anyone could imagine.

"I'm dead," he said, shocked to realize he could speak in water. Bubbles exited his mouth as he spoke and rose in front of his eyes. "I just died! I am dead, but I am alive and breathing! I am breathing underwater!" He was shouting as the bubbles rushed upward. "Why am I breathing if I am dead?"

He looked around. Several small fish surrounded him, nibbling gently at his skin. It felt good, like when his mom used to tickle his arm in church as a boy. They looked like sardines, but they had a strange fin that moved in a circular motion above their bodies and a split tail that moved up and down in opposite movements like swimming flippers. When one would dart off, the top fin would change motion in a sweeping pattern that propelled them away.

David moved his arms and they all darted away, disappearing into the water. A large creature with long piercing teeth in a permanent grin swam in slow motion toward David. The creature was as large as David. The teeth looked like the grill on a car as it got closer. The body of the fish appeared to be red metallic and the fins on the bottom were round, circulating like rotating black tires. Its eyes began to glow like headlights.

Again, David became confused. Maybe he was hallucinating and wasn't quite dead yet. As the creature got closer, David could see its red metallic scales were as large as his hands. He reached out to touch them as it glided by with its steady grin. The scales were as smooth as metal and felt as hard. Suddenly, the fish unfolded wing-like fins on its side and rose gracefully above him exposing a glistening silvery bottom with the black rotating fins still turning, moving the creature higher.

David moved his wings to follow the creature. As David followed, he began to see the water growing lighter. The creature turned, folded its wings, and dipped back past him slowly returning to the depths. David watched as it disappeared into the deep. He continued his ascent into the clear water above.

He wasn't sure if he wanted to surface just yet and decided to explore, straightening his body parallel to the surface. He swam forward. In front of him, several yards ahead, he could see a most beautiful reef. Purple, orange, red, yellow, and blue plant-like creatures beckoned in the currents of the water as he passed into a school of brightly striped fish. They only moved slightly to allow him entry rather than dart away as he expected.

The school opened up in front of him. He was surrounded by corals, anemones, rocks of purple and red, and swarms of brightly-colored fish. It seemed every color in the spectrum was in front of him at once. Above, the bright white light caused the bubbles rising around him to appear fluorescent.

Once again, David could only think of his mother. What she would give to be in an aquarium like this! To his right, David could see a pool of massive bubbles. The bubbles sounded like an orchestra of music that roared louder as he winged his way upward and over toward them. As he neared the surface, the sound began to form a clear roar, "I am…"

David's head popped upward out of the water to see the source of the bubble pool. Above him, cascading down a towering cliff was a waterfall singing clearly the familiar sound, "I am…"

David looked around. He was in a bay surrounded by towering cliffs. The cliffs had veins of a silvery and sparkly substance that glistened in the bright light as the water sprayed on them from the rocky edges where the waterfall spilled over.

He searched for a way out. There was no beach. He was encompassed by water on all sides, water and towering cliffs. He attempted to stretch his wings to glide through the water to find some place to exit. He could no longer feel them. He jerked his head around to look. His wings were gone!

David leaned his head back allowing the spray of the waterfall to moisten his already wet face. He closed his eyes in the bright light and stayed there treading water. Once again, he found himself smiling. He listened with his soul to the sound of the music from the bubbles and the roaring, "I am…" of the cascading water.

The water was not warm or cold. It was perfect. The air was clean and salty. He filled his lungs deeply. He opened his eyes as he realized that his lungs were filling with air. He was dead and breathing. Or was he? He pinched himself hard to see, screaming at his own abuse, "OW!" He wasn't dead, unless you can feel pain when you're dead!

He continued to tread water wondering at his trip through the ocean, his flight on disappearing wings, and he smiled again.

"Why not," he shouted at the waterfall. "Why not? Anything is possible, right? I believe it now!" David swam closer to the water fall. "I believe it now! You are awesome!" David realized his friend, who had so recently laughed at him talking to the rock would really laugh now. He was shouting at a waterfall!

"You are awesome!" He shouted as loud as he could.

"I am…"

The waterfall continued to repeat itself over and over splashing the top of the water with continual bubbles and foam that sung to David late into the evening. He continued to tread water. The water began to cool. His arms and legs grew tired.

Once, David tried to swim to the edge of the cliff, only to return to same spot. It seemed there was no way out. He wondered how long he would be able to continue to tread water before he grew too tired to stay afloat. He imagined himself giving up and slowly sinking to his death.

"What am I thinking?" he was talking to the waterfall again. "I just sank a while ago and here I am alive. Geez," he whispered with a disgusted tone. "I have to be the most …" He didn't finish.

He shook his head in self-disgust. He thought about his recent experiences and his repeated lack of trust. He remembered the doubt that had arisen so quickly and the fear that had been so dramatically overcome in one miraculous experience after another. He cringed at the instant unbelief that so easily beset him. David could only wonder at his human state. “What on earth is wrong with me?”

He turned to the waterfall addressing it with a directness that surprised even him. “What on earth is wrong with me? Why, after all these experiences, do I still get afraid? Why does that panic rise up in me at the moment I have no control over anything?”

Even as he spoke it, the realization was plain to him. He *needed* to be in control. He did not really know how to trust even after all he had already gone through. He could reason all he wanted. He could remember the experiences as clearly as if he were reliving them. They had felt realer than what he knew as real.

He had faced falling through the sky to the earth. He had sunk to the depth of the deep and allowed his lungs to fill knowing death should be imminent. He had soared through space. He had visited heaven and even earth in different time periods. He had seen the end and the beginning. He had walked and talked with God in the evening. Yet, here he was facing the possibility of death, and fear had poked up its ugly head again.

“What is wrong with us? Why does fear take control at the point we lose it?”

He floated, treading water as it grew darker and colder. Even the recognition that so far he hadn’t died could not help him. He struggled to find an escape from the sure possibility of sinking into the deep again.

Confusion over his inability to conquer his own human nature overwhelmed him. It seemed that God was able to rescue him in the direst of circumstances. He could remember that God could miraculously keep him alive in the most bizarre moments. Yet, he could still feel that desperate urge to avoid death.

He was still afraid of what he could not control himself. He still felt alone when the dark closed in. The sound of the waterfall began to sound like water, and the "I am…" began to fade from the air. The bubbles were bubbling and splashing; the music lost in the old, familiar sound of water.

His legs were growing stiffer as time passed. He was beginning to shiver. Fear gripped him as he struggled to fight it. "Why?" He shouted at the waterfall, but really to himself. "David!" he shouted at himself.

He screamed his own name louder and louder attempting to gain control over his own fear and emotions. His legs were becoming difficult to move; his arms were stiff and cold. The dark water was rising up over his chin, getting closer to sucking him into the cold and dark depth.

He screamed his own name again certain he could pull his emotions together. It only made things feel more ominous. His head bobbed under the splashing waves that seemed to be growing in size.

Surfacing long enough to screech out a moan, he went under again a little farther and longer this time. He was holding his breath, trying to remember how he had focused before. He couldn't find that face in his mind again. He was cold. He was beginning to lose all feeling in his body. A bobbing wave lifted his head long enough for him to screech out a weak, "Help!" His head bobbed under before he could take another breath. Panic shot through his soul for a brief second as he felt himself being lifted from the water by his shirt.

David instinctively grabbed the hands lifting him, almost pulling his rescuer into the water with him. Another pair of hands grasped his arms and helped to drag him into a small boat, scraping his torso as he was pulled from the water. With the top half of his body draped over the edge and his face lying on the gritty wet floor of the small boat, he felt himself being lifted and shoved completely in.

He was exhausted from fear and from treading the cold water for hours. He allowed himself to be dragged in completely and turned over onto his back. David's face was stinging from being scratched along the boat's bottom. He laid there with his breath coming in painful heaves. He tried desperately to catch his breath. The small effort of helping his rescuers to pull him up had seemed to pull the very life from him. Finally, he choked out a stuttering, "Thank you!"

There were only two men in the boat. Both nodded to David. David let out a sigh. He was cold. He was grateful. He was confused. "Who am I?"

He was still disgusted with his own inability to trust even after experiencing the miraculous. "Who am I?" He whispered it to the voice, to the waterfall, to God, and to the men who answered by looking at each other in questioning stares. They covered David with a tarp, wrapping his body to keep out the wind that was increasing and causing the small vessel to rock to the point of tipping.

David allowed himself to be lulled by the rocking. He thanked God silently for once again rescuing him. David lifted his head at the sudden shout of one of the seamen. A wave crashed over the small vessel causing it to fill with water and tip entirely over. David felt himself go under. He struggled to surface. He reached for the capsized boat and grabbed on desperately looking around for the two men. "Hey!" He could barely cough it out.

David heard splashing off to his right and could see both men just a few feet away swim in to grab the vessel as desperately as he had. Another wave crashed over them as they struggled to hold on. They were talking to each other in a strange language.

Another wave crashed, and as soon as it had passed, one of the men reached and pulled himself up to the top of the boat's bottom, which was now above him. Then, he reached to help David up, throwing his arm around and under his shoulder to help hold him to the top. The other man swam to David's other side and grabbed the top of the boat, which once had been the bottom. He pulled himself up and grasped the arm of the other man, helping to hold onto David.

David was completely overcome with emotions, the cold, and the efforts of these strangers to help him. The night swirled around him and he fell unconscious once again.

Chapter 10

David began to awaken slowly. He could feel himself bobbing up and down in a rhythmic motion. His arms and legs were tingling painfully. Pain seared through him as he tried to move. He wiggled his toes and pain shot through him again. He lifted his head and looked around. He was lying on the topside of a small boat floating upside down.

His arms and legs were hanging down over the side. He wiggled them again and moaned as the blood began to flow. He kept wiggling until the pain had subsided enough for him to move his arms from their deadened hanging weight to a position where he could lift his upper body. It hurt desperately. Still, he forced himself up to a sitting position, his deadened legs tingling in every movement.

He sat still for a few second trying to get his bearings, wiggling his legs slightly to aid the awakening process. He looked behind and all around in the surrounding water. He could not see the two men who had rescued him and left him safely on top of the capsized vessel. "Hello!" It was a weak call. He could see for quite a distance all around. There was no one.

"Hello?" His voice was strained. Had his rescuers died saving him? David squinted his eyes and held his hands to guard them from the light as he strained to see in the distance, searching for any possible movement. There was none. The water was still, barely lapping against the side of the small capsized boat.

David sat there wiggling his toes until he could fully feel them and the tingling had subsided enough to move them. He bent his legs and placed his feet against the sides of the boat and rubbed them as life began to flow painfully through them.

The sun was warming his body. A shiver ran down his back and arms in response. The sun felt good. He felt anxious and sad as he looked around searching the water close and in the far distance against the cliffs. They looked very small from this place in the lapping waves.

He leaned forward cautiously using his right arm as a paddle to turn the boat around in the direction of the cliffs and the waterfall. Once he had the boat turned, he began to paddle with both arms. He paddled until he was too tired to continue, all the while searching the gentle lapping waves for any sign of the men who had rescued him.

Slowly, throughout the day, he made his way to the waterfall. Every now and then, he stopped along the way searching the distant water. Once in a while, in great tiredness of body and soul, he stopped, looked around, and then closed his eyes in silent requests for God to help them wherever they were. Tears dropped now and then as he realized his own worth compared to theirs.

These two men had rescued him, not thinking about their own safety. He had gone through so many miracles and rescues. Still, he had only been desperately attempting to rescue himself and help them get him to safety. More and more,

David was beginning to feel that his own ways were not as honorable and selfless as he had always thought they were.

He felt selfish and thankless, filled with doubt and fear. He would have argued this up until this moment. He remembered with conviction the many times he had judged others as being faithless and selfish. He had been so sure of himself. He had been so sure of his ability to face fear and overcome it. He had felt he was pretty well in control of his own emotions. He argued about his ability to make choices when it was hard.

He had never really been put to a test like the ones he had recently experienced. Yes, he'd had fearful moments he had worked through. He had experienced hard times and even overcome many difficulties. He had never before faced the actual point of death and complete loss of control.

Even in that, he could have argued that he had faced it well. But, when death came looming again, he had found himself once again fearful. He had found he could breathe underwater when he gave in and trusted the face of Jesus. When death came taunting him with the possibility of drowning again and the cold had numbed him and darkness had overtaken him, he had been afraid and struggled to even find faith. He was no different than anyone else.

He had not just lived with others failing him. Now, he had to live with failing himself. This was hard to accept. Truthfully though, he had known it somewhere deep inside beyond the defenses he voiced and the attempts he had made at being good.

He had known that when it came right down to it, he was really nothing very special on his own. His life had been a pursuit to prove that wrong, more to himself than to anyone else. He had spent countless nights imagining having great wealth and even fame. Yes, he had to admit it. He had desired to be recognized as smart, important, and more than what he felt he really was. He had been sure that meeting with God would be that change that made him different. He had hoped for a miraculous immunity to the humanness of his own existence.

In the end, he was left with just that. He was nothing on his own. He had nothing of his own. Every breath, every moment, every experience rested on the intervention of something beyond himself. His only real recognition would come from someone bigger than himself.

He hung his head. He felt the reality of his own weakness deeper than ever. He had met with God. He had heard His voice. He had talked with Him and traveled eternity with Him. Yet, he was no better off than before. He was David. The moments of power and beauty, the moments of life and joy, and the miraculous and supernatural experiences were so far beyond him.

Yes, they were there. He had touched them and lived them; but, they were beyond him. They had been there for the asking. They were his when he believed, but his only because of someone else. David himself was just a thought, existing, living, surviving, and being only because of someone else who made it so.

The thought humbled him. It made him feel empty. His body felt limp and without any substance. He was poured out and tired to the bone. The sun beat down on him warming his limbs and drying his skin.

He spoke to himself as he looked up, "I exist only because…"

"I am…"

David looked up to see the waterfall just ahead. He smiled a humble, lop-sided smile and nodded at the waterfall as a gesture of understanding.

"I exist because you are."

David felt the conviction and desperation lift. He was only beginning to understand the ways of the One, who His very thought, created his existence. His ways were not David's ways. David's ways at their very best could not compare with His. He was nothing, a mere thought outside of Him. He felt completely powerless at that moment. Yet, right then, it felt good. It felt very, very good.

The lapping waves slowly moved him closer to the waterfall. As it grew closer, the sound of "I am…" grew louder and louder filling his spirit through and through. He breathed in deeply, lifting up his face and his very soul, tasting the sound of the voice of many waters pouring down over his face and the vessel he sat on.

The boat bobbed and moved, gently tipping and bowing as it floated under the waterfall, and then through it. David sat with his eyes closed, his face uplifted, and his arms outstretched.

The sound of the waterfall slightly faded as David passed through. Once inside, he saw he had entered a large cave-like structure. The waterfall was behind him, closing him off from the bay. Inside, the water was still and quiet. This seemed unusual with the waterfall creating such a splashing and turning of waters on the outside. But then, everything was unusual lately. Unusual was the only thing usual.

The pool of water was a deep, emerald green. The inside of the cave behind the waterfall was much like the cliffs on the outside, gleaming with veins of some sparkling substance and silver streaks that glistened with moisture. It would have been dark but for the light that cut through the waterfall in sharp, sword-like rays. They illuminated the walls and the emerald water.

David felt a strange sense of security as he floated on the still water. He looked down through the emerald green and saw that it was not very deep. The bottom was covered with rounded large boulders, very unlike the sharp edges surrounding him. He reached over to feel the water with his hand. It felt strangely warm and soothing.

He looked around to be sure he was safe from any strange creature lurking in the cave waters. "There I go again!" he thought, deciding not to be afraid. He let his feet drop. He was not going to be afraid! He pulled his feet back up, hugged his knees, and then swung his feet to one side lowering himself into the green depth. The bottom wasn't as close as it had seemed.

He lowered himself deeper into the water until it was up to his chin and his feet could feel the rounded boulders at its depth. He stretched his neck up, and with one hand, he held the edge of the boat, pulling it as he carefully stepped over the boulders. They felt smooth and comfortable as he stepped on them, moving deeper into the cave. The water grew shallow as he continued until he was walking up and out of it onto a beach of soft sand. The smooth boulders were scattered here and there on the beach at the back of the cave.

David walked to one of the larger ones after pulling the boat up and out of the water, dragging it onto the sand. He sat down rubbing his hands down his legs to squeeze out some of the water from his jeans. He took off his shirt and wrung it several times trying to get it as dry as possible. He looked up at the waterfall where it fell at the entrance of the cave. It looked as if it were changing form. He watched as the water fell, forming what began to look like a huge translucent hand.

David stared at it for a long time. He leaned against the boulder stretching his body to its full length, lying on his back. He continued to stare at the huge hand now covering the cave's opening. It was comforting. It made him feel covered and protected. The air was moist and warm.

The emerald water had been much warmer than the water outside the cave and had warmed his body up to his chin. A ray of sun shooting through and into the cave fell across him like a blanket. He had put his wet shirt back on to protect his back from the sand. He lied there, just staring at that protecting hand and listening to the faded music and the soft roar of "I am…" The gentle sounds lulled him into a restful and deep sleep.

He dreamed of the waterfall and the hand. He dreamed that the morning had come again and light was shining through. The form of a person was developing in the light. He dreamed that he sat up and reached out his arms. The form stepped forward and he saw his mother, smiling and passing through the waters. In his dream, he called, "Mom! Mom! Come in! Wait till I tell you about everything! Mom…." The dream faded and David opened his eyes. He sat up rubbing his eyes and missing his mother and his whole family very much.

He stretched and stood up feeling strong and whole. He saw his clothes were dry and unwrinkled. In fact, they looked clean. His skin looked moist and supple. Everything seemed clear and bright. He took in a long breath that felt very healing. He held it in for a few seconds, and then let it out slowly.

David wondered at the soft, baby-like feel of his skin. He felt his face. There was definitely hair growth. He looked around feeling strangely well. He looked at the deep, emerald pool and wondered if the water had made him feel that way. He felt whole and healed, comforted and content. He wondered if the warmth he felt physically had actually warmed his soul, or vice versa.

He took off his clothes looking around to be sure no one was hiding in this sanctuary he had discovered. He stepped carefully into the emerald green water and walked on the smooth boulders deeper and deeper until it was up to his chin once more. He stood there for minutes, balancing by holding his arms out to his side. Slowly, he lowered his head under the water allowing it to completely engulf him. He held his breath as long as he could.

Remembering his recent experience, he took in a breath under the water as he had in the deep sea. Pain shot through his lungs and he shot up out of the water sputtering and coughing.

Once he had regained his composure, he took another deep breath, coughed again, and went under. This time he held his breath the entire time. He came up and went back down a third time, staying under as long as he could. He came up, tossed the water from his hair and walked slowly up and out again to the sandy beach. He tried to wipe off any excess water he could. He shook himself like a dog after a bath. He walked around in the cave for a while, put his clothes back on, and then sat on the boulder. He was no longer tired, but he was very hungry.

He leaned down looking into the water. He couldn't see any fish. He wouldn't be able to catch any if he did; but, it just seemed like the right thing to do. He walked around the entire beach at the back of the waterfall. There was nothing resembling plants or anything that could be eaten.

The sound of voices stopped David from searching further. He listened. He could hear the water and the bubbles. He could faintly hear the voice in the waters. He could make out the music; but, there was something more he had heard. There it was again! There were voices and laughter. Yes, it was definitely voices! Before he could move to run to the water, several men came shooting through the water sitting on the broken trunk of a large tree, all leaning forward and paddling with all their strength into the emerald green pool. David stood speechlessly watching them.

They were breathless and seemed to be in a hurry. Their voices were merry and filled with laughter despite the evident rush to get inside. Once inside, they laughed softly and whispered. Paddling carefully and quietly to the middle of the pool, the men motioned to each other to be quiet. They all slid quietly off the log and into the water.

They were carrying packs on their backs and swords were slung across their sides. They were dressed in tunics and had their heads bound in cloth, wrapped and tied with multicolored ropes. All wore a sash that draped across their torsos diagonally and tied at their sides hanging loosely, opposite the side with the swords. All had beards and dark curls hanging from under the banded turbans.

David was very still, unsure of what to do. He had no place to run. As they came up out of the water and walked closer to the edge, David could see they were muscled, rough looking, and they walked with an intimidating stride. The swords only made them seem more ominous! Still, he had no choice but to stand there or get in the water and walk out to them. He opted to stand until they noticed him. As they stepped out of the water, the largest of them looked up, noticing David on the far side. He stopped short, his hand reaching for his sword.

David felt himself draw in a quick breath. Again, there he was facing that instant fear, that panic that just overwhelms you even when you have just experienced a miracle! He could feel the panic and the hatred of it at the same time. He had no power over it.

The moment the man reached for his sword, another reached to stop him, looking straight at David. He smiled. Heading straight toward David, he walked out of the water, and then around the edge of the beach. His fellows were following closely behind, all looking straight at David. The man stopped a few feet from David and lifted his hand, stopping the men behind him. He was obviously their leader. The man stood there for what seemed an eternity to David. He looked at David with a strange smile. Then, he sat down on the rock signaling his men to follow suit, looking away as if David did not even exist.

David stayed put. The men all sat at their leader's command; but they kept their eyes on David. They did not look friendly at all, or amused as did their leader.

The man took out a long knife from a pouch at his side. He pulled it out and looked at it closely, rubbing his fingers lightly along the edges as if to feel its sharpness. He did not look back at David, but spoke in a loud voice.

"Friend! Come on over and join me. Sit here on this rock," he said patting a large round boulder next to the one he was seated on. David stood still, trying to make his body respond to what his mind was telling him to do. He tried to make his legs move to obey the command of this man sitting there stroking a knife. David looked at the other men glaring at him. Some still stood with their hands across their bodies resting on their swords, ready to pull them out at the first command.

"Friend!" It was said sharper this time. "Come on over here!" He patted the boulder again. "Sit on this rock and tell me what it is thinking." The other men all turned to look at their leader in surprise at the same time. "Come on over and tell me what this rock has to say!" It was a strong command; but, David heard the humor and a lilt in the voice.

David's body twitched in a forward movement and the leader stood, turning to look at him. He had a smile and a look of friendliness that seemed welcoming. David still couldn't move. "You still talk to rocks, don't you?" He was obviously enjoying his joke from the look on his face.

"David?" David moved forward asking his question. "David?" He was repeating himself again. He was very confused. The boy he had left just a day or two ago was standing in front of him as a man. It seemed impossible. "But then, so does everything lately!" David was talking out loud to himself without realizing it.

"David!" He knew it was him. He recognized the dark, olive-colored eyes and the smile. Flashes of the young boy's friendly face shot through David's memory, as did the recollection of the three men he had danced with at the first part of this journey.

"David!" He ran forward to the leader, reaching to grab him as the other men pulled their swords. David stopped short. The leader held up his hand again, not looking at his men, but instead staring directly at David with an amused smile.

"It has been a long time, my friend. Tell me, do you still talk to rocks? I need to know what this one has to say to me before I lay my head on it to rest. Will it mind? Please ask it if I can rest on it." His smile grew showing straight white teeth. He had grown into a very handsome man.

David smiled back. With a deep bow from the waste and a sweeping hand, David stated with feigned seriousness, "My Friend and King, I shall ask the rock for you at your request!" David walked to the boulder and knelt down beside it getting closer, whispering to it.

The men who had put their swords back at rest were watching as if they thought both David and his old friend were crazy. David was enjoying the game. "Rock," he spoke in a loud whisper. "Pray, tell me, might this shepherd king rest his head upon you tonight?"

David turned his ear to the rock, waiting for a few seconds, and then jerked back as if in shock. "What? But, well, why would you wish that?" David moved away from the rock standing up in pretended sorrow and bowing again. "My Friend and King, I am sorry to deny you the rest you so wish. But, the rock has spoken and informed me that only I may rest my head upon it. You will have to sit at my side and sing me to sleep. Only then may you join me in rest."

Smirking playfully at the shocked but amused look on the leader's face, David turned and lied down, resting his head on the boulder with a huge and exaggerated sigh, closing his eyes.

The leader smiled and reached inside his tunic taking out a hand-made flute. He stroked the instrument, gliding his fingertips along its smooth sides. His face grew more serious. He closed his eyes and lifted his face in silence taking in a long, slow breath. He was completely absorbed in the moment. The men had been staring at their leader. They were evidently confused at his behavior. When he pulled out the instrument, they grew reverently still, intently watching him with anticipation in their eyes.

The young man raised the instrument slowly and purposefully to his lips. Taking in a deep breath first, he blew gently into the flute. The sound vibrated and sent chills down David's spine. The hollow notes became a part of his being and he found his deepest emotions stirred. He imagined floating into the very sound of the flute. The tune continued filling his soul, becoming one with him. He felt as if he was floating on the notes of the flute, weightless and dreamily.

David had no other feelings at that moment. Gone were the anxieties of the day. Gone were the memories of distant and recent past. He felt the absence of sorrow and anger as each note trimmed away the dead edges of loss, rejection, anger, doubt, sorrow, and every negative emotion or thought with sharp precision. He was as peaceful and relaxed as he had ever been. There were no words or thoughts that could explain or describe the experience. This music was healing his spirit.

The flute sung into the night hours, long past when the men had drifted off to sleep on the trilling notes of the shepherd's instrument. David lie as still as those lost in a world of dreams. He listened to the hollow notes rising and falling and sending chills through him. The sound of the flute ended in one long, low, vibrating note.

He heard the leader lie down on the sand. David peeked to see what he was doing. The leader had laid his head on the sand. He had placed his hands under his own head to support it. He began to sing a soft and quiet song.

The voice was sweet, as beautiful as it was when the leader was a young boy. David listened to the words. They spoke of fears, sorrows, wonderings, and troubles. The words brought tears to David's eyes. He understood the cry of the heart in the words. He had felt the very things this friend of his was singing. He swallowed hard.

David could hear in the words that this other David was singing his soul as well. The words turned to grateful praises for all God had rescued him from. He sang of hopes and dreams. The words were soothing and healing. He sang of the feelings David had recently felt. He sang of miracles. He sang about fear. He sang about the futility of man without God. He sang of the wonder that God noticed man. He sang of his own humility in the presence of a God so big, and yet so personal.

David was still, breathing quietly and taking in every word. The young leader stopped singing and turned to look at David, leaning closer to see if he had sung him to sleep. David was far from sleep. He held still, keeping his eyes closed. The young leader moved away cautiously trying not to awaken his friend. David carefully opened his eyes just a bit. Even in the dark of the cave, David could see him standing there.

The moonlight was beaming in through the waterfall just enough to outline his form. He stood there like a statue. The men were all as still as David. He wondered if they were sleeping or just pretending they were, as he was. He continued to watch as the young leader walked around the men looking at each one as they lie there in the sand.

Again, he began to sing softly. He sang a prayer of peace, protection, and blessings as he walked around the men in his company. He sang for at least another hour. David lied still, watching and listening to the words and the beautiful voice. He wondered if the men were listening to their leader pleading for their safety and blessing.

Finally, David could see him walking back to his spot. The young man sat down and leaned his back against the rock wall, facing the waterfall. He sat there humming softly. Eventually, his voice faded off. David took a long, slow breath and let his own mind drift off into a blissful sleep.

Chapter 11

David dreamed. He dreamed of swimming through giant anemones and coral. Huge, blue fish swam and caressed him with their fins. Colorful rainbows spiraled in the water world of his dream. He swam into one spiral that took him around and around and carried him upward like a tornado. He rose higher and higher.

He could see large sharks, dolphins, fish, and plants swirling as he spiraled up and past them. He surfaced, riding the top of a huge wave that just stood there, defying gravity. He could see another wave cresting in front of him, but in the distance. It too was holding its place, having risen to the same height, wet and majestic like the one David was riding.

He looked down, surprised to see a road between the two waves. It was sandy and dry with rocks and gravel running between his wave and the one cresting in front of him. David could see many people, sheep, cattle, and carts to his left traveling off the road and coming up onto a bank. "This must be the parting of the Red Sea and that must be the people of Israel passing out of it," he thought out loud.

Even as he said it, he realized what he had just said, "Passing out of it!" He turned quickly to look to the right as he saw an army of chariots and horses entering from the other side at full speed!

"Oh, no!" David shouted just as the wave fell and he found himself rolling and tossing about in a flurry of water and bodies. His arms were flailing. His feet were kicking, trying to fight the water and objects. His eyes suddenly flew open as he awakened from his watery dream, realizing he was flailing about and something was over his mouth. It was a hand! He jerked about trying to get air and to free himself when he heard a whisper.

"Be still and I'll let you go! Quiet!" David stopped moving and the hand was removed with a whispered reminder, "Quiet!" An arm was wrapped around his middle gently. It was very slowly pulling him backwards and deeper into the back of the dark cave.

David could see as he was moved backward the outlines of men in the front of the cave close to the waterfall on the other side. He could hear voices and laughter. David wondered what was happening. He trusted the arm moving him back. He was sure the whispered voice was his friend's voice. He wondered if his friend was playing a trick on his men, or if his men had turned on him and he was trying to hide. As they touched the very back of the cave wall, the arm pulled him down and they crouched there. David felt the weight of someone beside him, crouching as well. He held still not knowing what else to do. They stayed in that position until David's legs were cramping.

He must have unconsciously moved slightly because the arm tightened around his waist in a jerked warning. He held as still as he could in response. David's legs began to shake from cramping. The men at the front of the cave had lied down long before. He thought he could hear snoring and a cough or two.

David wondered what was next. If this was a game, his legs hurt too badly to continue; and, if it were danger of some sort, it still hurt too much. David held still, with the arm wrapped around him. He felt the arm around him tug him upward from the cramped position.

A hand came over his mouth again. This time, it was held lightly in a gesture to silently remind him to stay quiet. David nodded to let his friend know he understood. He stood on dead, shaking legs. He could not have stood on his own. He was surprised his friend could stand up from such a position, let alone help him as well.

The arm tugged at him to move him around so he was no longer walking backward. They edged their way along the back of the cage moving cautiously around to the side, and then continued through the edge of the waterfall where they exited the cave. The sound of the waterfall deafened the sound of their escape, leaving the sleeping men snoring to the rhythm of the water's musical fall as they passed through it.

David could see in the moonlight that men were passing through ahead of them, and once through, others were following. Silently, the wet crew scrambled over slippery rocks, and then off and up to the right, climbing higher. When they reached the top edge where the water began its descent, they stopped to rest. No one spoke a word. They sat silently, still dripping and chilled from the night air. The young leader had aided David's ascent the entire way.

Now, he walked to the edge of the waterfall looking down. He stood there for several minutes. He unsheathed a sword, held it high, and then returned it to its place. He turned and the men stood, following him off into the inky darkness away from the waterfall and into the woods.

David stumbled along behind his friend, tripping and falling several times in the dark. His legs were no longer numb. They ached badly and the night air chilled him through his wet clothes. His teeth began to chatter. His body was shaking hard. No one else was complaining or making any sound. Only David's teeth and his slipping and falling along the way gave any evidence of the escaping small army of men as they passed through the darkness to safety. David was embarrassed. He tried hard to keep his footing. He tried to hold his teeth still, and when that didn't work, he held his mouth open. His jaws were aching. They felt like they would lock any second from the shaking of his mouth and the cold, stiffened muscles of his jaws.

The men walked on, not stopping once throughout the night. As the day began to break, he could see that the men were all there. They were looking back and all around as they marched on through the trees and bushes. When daylight broke through, the leader stopped and raised his hand.

Everyone stopped. No one made a sound. They all listened. The only sounds were from birds and bugs. He heard the cry of an eagle. Then, he heard a sound like a twig crack off to his right. He could hear his heart pounding in his ears and head. He wasn't sure what the danger was. He was sure there must be something very sinister they were moving away from.

Another crack! A small deer stepped out in front of them obviously surprised to see the silent men. It was too late. One of the men had lodged an arrow into a bow and had let it fly. The arrow hit its mark. The deer fell with a very light thud, almost making no sound at all. The men stood still and quiet for a few seconds longer.

One of the men pulled the arrow from the animal's body. Handing the bloodied arrow to the man who had shot it, he lifted up the small limp animal and tossed it over his shoulders. He silently moved on through the forest. Everyone followed without a word. They walked along until they came upon some heavy brush. At this point, they all stopped, looked around and behind them, holding still to listen again. Then, pulling back some of the bushes, two of the men exposed an entrance to a dark cave. They held back the bushes for the men to pass through. David and the leader stepped inside first, and then the rest followed. Then, the bushes were placed back carefully covering the cave and shutting out the light completely. For the first time throughout the entire night, David heard his friend's voice whisper.

"Come." He tugged at David's arm. They walked into the cave deeper and deeper. It grew darker as they went. David was relying on the hand clutching his arm to lead the way. Finally, they stopped. The hand tugged David down to the ground and he heard a whispered, "Rest, Friend!"

It didn't sound like a suggestion. It was a command. David lied down and closed his tired eyes. He was drier. The air in the cave was cool, but not as cold as the night air had been. He had stopped shivering. The hike had warmed his blood. The exertion had exhausted him. He fell into a deep, and this time, dreamless sleep.

David was awakened by the stirring of the men around him. He must have been asleep for several hours. He felt rested. His clothes were dry. It was still very dark in the cave.

"Come, David." He felt a hand gripping his arm in an effort to help him stand. As he stood, he was instructed in a low voice. "It's time to go." He was pulled forward, and then left to walk on his own. David reached to feel his friend in front of him, in order to keep from running into him, and followed him to the entrance of the cave. As they stepped out, the moon shed light on the men. David was able to see clearly even though night had fallen once again. The darkness of the cave had allowed his eyes to adjust. The moon made everything seem as clear as day. He was able to follow as the men walked on through the trees and bushes.

After a brief walk, they came out of the trees. David could see his friend's face clearly. He wanted to ask what had happened and why they were traveling at night. He wanted to ask where they were going. He was trying to remember the stories he had heard as a child about this David who was a king. He remembered something about him running from another king. He had heard a story about him hiding in caves and leading a band of rough fellows who were very loyal to him. He wished he had read the Bible more. He wished he had paid more attention to the stories his mother had shared with him. David had stopped watching where he was going. His mind was struggling to remember.

Suddenly, he ran into a large, dark object. He reached out to feel it. It had a strange smell and felt furry and warm. He could feel the hair on his neck prickle and his heart pounding. He had run into a beast of some sort. He was afraid to move. The object moved away from him with a low, grunting sound. David stood still. He wasn't sure what to do. Fear was gripping his heart and he felt light-headed. He wanted to call out to his friend. He was afraid to make a sound, both because of the beast and because it was obvious the men were trying to be stealthy. He didn't want to bring danger to them. His breaths became short and labored. He was trying to keep his breathing from being loud. He couldn't stop the heaving sounds. The night began to swirl around him and he dropped to the ground with a soft thud.

"David! Come!" The voice was still almost a whisper but carried a command that stirred David to move. "Get up! Come!" The words were sharp and demanding. David rose quickly and held onto his friend's clothing, following him silently. He wished to explain what had just happened. He didn't want his friend to think he was weak and had just dropped from exhaustion. He wanted to explain about the beast. Then, the realization that this was the one who had killed a lion as a youth raced through his mind. He would not be helping his reputation with his friend by being so afraid of an animal that he had almost passed out.

They continued to walk throughout the night. When the first rays of the sun broke through the darkness again, causing the morning sky to glow in a rosy-golden light, the leader stopped and stretched. He sat down on the ground crossing his legs. Some of the men did the same. Others scouted around the area first. The man carrying the deer removed it from his shoulders, allowing it to flop stiffly on the ground. He silently pulled out a sharp knife and began to remove the entrails and skin with the precision of a surgeon. Some of the others began to gather wood brush. They built a small fire and placed huge strips of venison on sticks turning them over the flames. It reminded David of roasting hotdogs.

The men ate silently after handing David a huge strip to roast himself. He turned it over and over till it was completely done. As he ate, he stared at the meat. He felt ashamed. He felt very childlike for having to be helped along. Tears were threatening to expose him even further. He fought to hold them back. He glanced up to see his friend. Their eyes met and David could see his friend's eyes were as full of tears as his. The leader looked away quickly, and then walked off and away from the men.

David was tired from the hike through the night. His body was warm from the fire. He stood and walked to his friend's side. He knew it was a daring move since this man had isolated himself from the others. The other men looked up. David could see they too thought it daring. He came up beside the other David who stood with tears flowing down his tan and dirty face, streaking it in muddy rivers. He glanced sideways at David but said nothing for a few seconds. Looking back at the horizon, he spoke lowly. "We were companions once. The man who follows me." Tears flowed. The broken and sorrowful look on his face sent a pain through David's heart as well. David nodded trying to show he understood. They sat there a long while silently watching the horizon. Tears flowed down the leader's face as he hummed to himself. David wiped his face every now and then, so touched by his friend's sorrow that his own brokenness was allowed to rush out in hot tears. They sat and wept silently together. Finally, the young man broke the silence. “What are you here for? Where did you go before?”

David stared at him. How could he explain he had grown wings and flown away, finding himself in another time? Years had passed for his friend. Only days had passed for David. “Do I look any older?’ David hoped this would help explain what he was about to share.

“Any older than what?’ the young man asked.

David looked down, smiling slightly at his friend’s ability to lighten the conversation. “…than when you first met me.” David was trying to match the quietness with which his friend spoke. “Do I look any older than I did when you were a boy?”

“That was a long time ago. I don’t know.”

“Well, I probably don’t.” David was playing with a blade of stiff grass he had pulled. “When I left…well, for me it was only a few days ago.” David was searching for words to explain.

“Where did you go? Where do you come from? Who are you, David?” The questions were quiet and sincere. David sighed and looked down at the blade of grass he was playing with. He shook his head slightly before answering.

“I’m not really sure who I am. I am sure not who I thought I was.” He paused, looked up at his friend, and then looked back down as he continued. “I mean…Well, a few…” David stopped again. He wasn’t sure what to say. He tried again.

“Well, what I think is a few days ago, I left my home. With all that has happened, I am not sure if it has only been a few days, or if it has been years, or centuries, or maybe even...” David was searching for words. He could see his friend was puzzled as he waited for David to explain. “I think I wanted to discover something, I guess. So I left and just started walking.”

“Discover? What did you want to find?”

“God, for one thing.”

“God? You left home to find God? Why?”

David looked up. “Why would I want to find God?”

“Why did you have to leave home to find Him? He is everywhere.”

David shrugged, “Well, I probably didn’t need to. I’m sure He was there. I needed to….I don’t know…get away from distractions.” His friend nodded as if understanding now. "I lived in a place called California. It's a long way from here, across the ocean on the other side of the world. But," David hesitated to continue. "But, it's not only far from here; it is also in a different time. I came from the future."

The young man looked at David. He looked him up and down, stopping to look at his wrapped feet. It was the same wrapping the young boy had wrapped his feet with many years before. It didn't look as if it had aged. "Looks like you came from the past."

"Well, I did. I mean… I came from the future first. Look, I know this really makes me look crazy. I am sure I seem more like a madman than ever. I was walking along this road. When I left home, you know?" David kept talking. "I was walking along, not sure where to go, or even if I should continue on or go back home. I had left home feeling unsatisfied with myself, or something. I just needed something different…something that felt more….well, real."

David realized he wasn't making any sense to his friend. In fact, he wasn't making sense at all. He had left home and everything he had ever known to be real to find reality. It didn't make sense when he tried to explain it. Now, he was living in what seemed unreal. Yet, it felt more real than what he was escaping from; while at the same time, it seemed surrealistic, impossible even. He wanted to explain.

His friend was quiet, waiting for him to continue. “I fell asleep on the side of a lane and night came. I woke up and saw a building in the dark. I went inside it and stuff started to happen…strange things. Like, well….I fell asleep inside the building and the next morning, woke up on the lane again; and, the building had disappeared. This happened over and over again, night after night. The building would appear at night. I would fall asleep inside it, and then I would wake up in the morning on that lane, that little dirt road, and the building would not be there.”

“Maybe you were dreaming.” David was glad that he was telling someone about this and that he was being listened to.

“That’s what I thought! But, one night I found a pencil in the building and I drew on a piece of paper and put it in my pocket.” David tucked his fingers in his pocket and pulled out the paper and pencil.

“When I woke up, I was on the lane again, and the building was gone, but the pencil and paper were still in my pocket as real as anything. From that time on, one strange thing after another happened! You see that drawing? That is an engine

I designed trying to pass time. I drew it while I was inside the building. When I woke up one morning on the lane again, it was still in my pocket."

"Engine?"

David thought for a few seconds. He wondered how to explain an engine to someone who had no knowledge of technology. "It is a machine. It is something with power to make things move like…" He stopped. Then, he said with revelation, "Like the wheels on a chariot or like a horse pulling a chariot." He stopped again, realizing there really was no way to describe an engine.

"Anyway," he went on. "It is something from my time. We have things like chariots, but they are called cars. You put one of these engines in them and you can make it go faster than…well, many times faster than your fastest horse or chariot. I like to draw them and try to design them to make cars go even faster, or to be more efficient." He realized he needed to get back on the subject while someone was listening.

"Anyway, I drew this engine to be very powerful. I was just imagining, you know, playing around to pass time. I drew it imagining it could go so fast it could take me through time, not just through space. Well, there in that building that kept appearing…" He stopped and started again. "I looked out and saw there was this vehicle, chariot thing, right out in the field where the building was."

David continued to tell the story. He told his friend about getting into the vehicle and finding himself growing older as he traveled through space, and then landing in the future somewhere. The more he talked, the more he realized how crazy it sounded. How could you travel into the future, aging as you went, and then end up younger in a future time?

"I think I traveled right through the future into Heaven because I aged as I went. I could see myself in the glass…in the reflection of this stuff inside the vehicle, like how you can see yourself in water. I grew a beard and my face got wrinkled as I went. I was getting older as I traveled and could see myself getting older. Then, when I landed, when I stopped I mean, I was younger than I was before. I didn't realize it at first. I didn't realize it till I actually saw my reflection in water later in this really beautiful place."

"I was in the most incredible place you can imagine. It had to be Heaven, you know, where God lives. Everything was alive. I mean everything! Trees were alive. They weren't just growing and living. They moved on their own. They danced. They moved sometimes in response to my voice."

David could see that his friend was listening without judgment. In fact, he looked anxiously at David to continue. There was a hungry longing in his eyes. He was leaning toward David to be better able to hear.

"Music was everywhere and it was alive, too. I don't know how to explain that." His friend just nodded in affirmation. "The water spoke. The wind breathed through my clothes causing it to dance. Not just like when the wind blows normally. It was purposeful. It was rhythmic, matching the music. It was as if the wind was using my clothes to dance through!"

"The grass massaged me. It was alive, rubbing against me and caressing me as I moved. I could walk… without touching the ground! Birds danced in the air. They sang songs with the wind."

The young leader let out a sigh and looked off. David stopped talking for a few minutes. His friend began to hum as he stared at the sky, and then began to sing.

"Birds find homes where you dwell,
sparrows find their place.
They raise their young and sing their songs,
as we sing of your grace.
God, my God the King!
How blessed to live and sing with you!"

David continued to explain the place he had visited. "I saw many children and young people there. They knew me and it felt like I knew them. But, I couldn't really place them." He looked at his friend's dark, olive-colored eyes and the beautiful complexion remembering the dance! David felt a lump in his throat. He stared at the young leader, trying to continue, but unable to utter a word. Tears stung his eyes and he swallowed hard. He looked intently into those dark eyes. "You were there." It was a whisper. "I danced with you there, and with Him."

The young leader did not take his eyes off David. He swallowed hard, the same way David had, and tears filled his eyes as well. They just looked at each other for a long time, till David looked down. Neither David talked for a while. After a long time had passed, the young man commanded David, "Tell me more."

"It was so beautiful there. I didn't want leave. I thought I must be dreaming and did not want to wake up! Sometimes, I wondered if I had died and gone there. There was this place I found there. It was like a castle on top of a high cliff. It was made of huge rocks. When I got up close to it, I saw it had been hand-carved on every piece of rock that it was built from. They were all carvings of my life, people I knew, places I had been, things I had done, memories carved into the stones. It was a place that had been hand-made for me.

Some of the carvings had me in them, but I couldn't remember them. I am guessing that they are things that will happen to me in the future. I must be going back to my time at some point to live them out. I am guessing I was in Heaven in the future, in a place made for me so I could remember the beautiful things of my life on earth. Looking at them there made them seem so much more real and so much more important. I haven't been very appreciative of my life or the experiences I have had.

I think I felt sorry for myself. I felt like I didn't have a life really. I had felt like my life had no substance or meaning and I felt empty. But, when I looked over the carvings and remembered how many things I had experienced…"

He stopped briefly. Then, he continued. "I have taken my life for granted I guess. I wasn't satisfied. I wanted more and didn't appreciate the moments that He cherished enough to carve into a memorial for me."

As he talked, he realized he was speaking more to himself than to his friend until his friend spoke, "Every breath we take is a treasure. Every moment is a place in eternity. It will all be carved into a memorial…each moment must be one of having been lived well." He was speaking to himself as well.

David stayed quiet as he continued. "Oh, let me rise in the morning and live always with you! Let the carvings in my memorial be ones with you! I will complete what I promised you I would do. I will do it with your people. When we arrive at death and see our memorials, you will welcome me. Oh my Lord, I am your servant! My mouth is full of praise for you. My heart is filled with your goodness. I am a joke to those who seek me. They shake their heads at my calamity. But, my life is precious in your sight. My moments are so important to you that you will honor me with a memorial of my times. You will remember me in the stones with which you will build me a dwelling place of safety. You will give me a banquet in front of them and I will dance with you in your house."

Again, the two were silent, as David reflected on his friend's thoughts and on his own. He was not at all like this David. He had not considered anything about his life as precious or as important as it really was. In fact, he had left his life because he had considered it so unimportant. Here was this friend of his sitting on a mountain, pursued, with nothing but a gang of rough men who had little more than the clothes they wore and he was reflecting on his life as something precious. After several minutes, the young man turned to David.

"Continue," he commanded.

"I saw a lot there. So much, it was unbelievable! Creatures like you could never imagine! They were all interested in me and responded to me. There was nothing to fear. You killed a lion when you were young." The leader looked down at the ground, and then looked back up at David.

"Yes."

"I ran with them and they were huge! They ran beside me and didn't try to hurt me. I saw this great beast like a dragon, white like a pearl with eyes of fire. It breathed fire, flew, and swam in the deep. Little children rode on him like a horse right through the depths. I could breathe underwater! Someday, I will ride him!"

"After there, I went back in time to the beginning…in the vehicle. I didn't want to leave where I was, but I did. I went to the beginning of time here on earth! I saw Adam and Eve and the Garden! I saw them take the fruit. I saw the serpent." David saw his friend shudder slightly. He was listening intently, so David continued.

"The Garden was much more beautiful than any paintings I have ever seen of it. People from my time are always trying to paint it like they imagine it to look. It was almost as alive as the first place I was in, Heaven, but not exactly. I saw Adam and Eve. I talked to God in the evenings."

His friend was hanging on his every word. David had always loved it when someone would listen to him.

"I didn't see Him. I didn't have a body, so nothing could see me, except Him obviously, because He talked to me. And, except…" David shuddered this time, "…except the serpent. He could see me. I know because he looked right at me. It sent chills through me, even though I didn't have a body. It was awful, that look!" David shuddered again.

"No body? You were there in your spirit."

"I guess. He said I was just a thought, but that I was real because I was His thought." David smiled, remembering.

"Before you were born, you were written in His book. He knew everything about you before you were conceived. You were real to Him."

The young leader spoke to David, and then gazed off at the distant horizon and spoke to someone who held his heart and his thoughts at that moment. "You are all I want here on earth. You will be all I want in the heavens. All the stages of my life were observed by you. You carved me out of nothing and made me something. All the days of my life were made before I was more than a thought to you, before I ever lived one day here."

David began telling him about the trip through space and seeing himself in contrast to the Christ. He began to weep, declaring with emphasis how different he was than the Messiah. He shared the stories of his childhood and how the Messiah had lived his in direct contrast to how David had.

He described the crucifixion and how he had been the one under the cross, weighted down under its heavy wood, beaten, sick, and feverish with no escape. He described how suddenly the cross had been lifted and he had been freed from the horror of pain and imminent death by someone who took his place for him. He described the beating. He described the bloodied and swollen eyes of the Messiah.

David could see the young man was thinking and struggling with what he was telling him. Then, he turned away and let out a moan as if feeling it himself as David continued. He turned back, waiting for David to go on.

He shared his feelings about the experience of watching the Messiah take his place in death after seeing the contrast of his guilty life compared to the Messiah's innocent life. He told of the sorrow he'd felt missing the beautiful voice in the Garden.

David told him how he had passed out and ended up in the vehicle, landing in the dessert by the rock where this David had found him as a boy. He shared about the confusion of hearing the voice from the rock in the desert. He described every detail of his flight with wings like eagles and his descent to the depths of the sea. He told in detail the miraculous interventions he had experienced.

His friend listened closely. Again, the young leader spoke, "Is there any place we could ever go to be away from Him? If you rode to the sky on wings, He would be there. If you dived to the depths of the deepest ocean, He would still be there with you. In the night, He sees you, immersed by His light. Height or depth, light or dark, they are all the same to Him. This is much too wonderful! I cannot take it all in!"

"Then, here I am with you again, years after the first time we met and you are a man. Yet, it has only been a very few days since I left you. You can see by my age and the wrappings on my feet that I am not telling you a lie! It's true. I don't know how this is all happening. I just keep finding myself in different times."

"Where will you go next?" He wasn't really asking David. He was wondering out loud. "I'd like to go. If I grew wings, I would fly to the heights of the wind and soar to Him." He began to hum to himself and lied back on the ground on his hands.

David thought about what he had said. "If he had grown wings, he would have flown away to God!" David felt scolded. He knew that the comment was not to scold him at all. It was from the heart of his friend. It had scolded him, however.

After all, it was David who was on some lofty search to find God. He hadn't thought one time about flying away to the heights of the wind to God.

David looked up at the sky. He had actually had wings, supernaturally-occurring wings! He probably could have done just that, but it hadn't even crossed his mind. He had enjoyed getting to fly. He had been focused on the experience of it all. He had tried to control it and make it work for him to get where he wanted to go. He had not thought of using it for the sole purpose of getting to God. David sighed. He had lived his life in just the same way, trying to control it and make it work for him to get where he wanted to go. His life had never been for the sole purpose of finding God. Even finding God had been for the sole purpose of serving his own desires.

Maybe his quest for answers to life, and for God, had nothing to do with getting away from distractions. Maybe he was fooling himself. What if it were as simple as just deciding to realize God in where he was and what he had? Maybe the biggest distraction in finding God was simply himself, his own desires, his need to control things and make them work for him. Maybe what he wanted was not God at all. Maybe God, to him, was just one more way to get to where and what he wanted. This friend wanted God. It was in his eyes, in his voice, and in the songs he sang.

David looked at the distant horizon. He could see something moving toward them. "Look!" He said, turning to his friend. The young leader was already staring in the direction David was pointing to. He nodded in response to David without saying a word. He sat there and watched for a while. David watched with him, glancing now and then at his friend's face. Sorrow lined the usually youthful expression. David would have named it "longing." He kept his thoughts to himself, as did the other David.

David was tired. He hadn't slept since yesterday, having travelled throughout the long night. Most of the men were dozing after their warmed meal. David noticed again the tired and wishful lines in his friend's face. He was obviously tired from exertion. After all, he had helped David many times while climbing. He had not slept as much as his companions. "Besides," David thought to himself, "He is sad."

David knew he was also lonely for his old friends that pursued him now. He had heard it in his comments and had seen it in the wistful expressions as he watched them climbing across the valley, where they had themselves ascended to the top previously. David was familiar with the feeling. He knew well how it felt to be lonely and sad for lost companionship. He understood the depth of fatigue that sorrow and loss can etch into your very being. He also knew he had no words of comfort though he wished for them. He had tried many times to comfort himself and had experienced the inability to even define the feelings, let alone solve them with words.

When the travelers across the ravine topped the other side and stopped to rest, the young man stood and walked to his companions, kneeling to stir them to wakefulness. As each sat up, he raised his hand slightly to silence them, and then pointed across the deep cavern to the other side. Each man rose silently. Some nodded, affirming they understood. Others just rose and began breaking camp, gathering their articles silently.

David helped to clean the site of their camp, brushing the area with a small branch to stir the ground and cover any evidence of their rest there. The young leader smiled at David, showing his approval. The entire troop was ready and moving in just a few minutes. They walked away from the edge and circled farther down to a place where they entered a small path that led through dense brush and trees.

Moving the brush back, they followed the path which began to open up wider as they walked a few yards. The brush had fallen back over the entrance so the path was no longer exposed to passer-by. These men knew the wilderness well. David and his friend followed two men who led the way. The rest of the gang followed bringing up the rear. David wondered if this was purposeful to protect their leader or if it had just happened that way.

As they worked their way down the valley, the young leader pushed his way through to the front leaving David behind the two men. He wanted to be next to his friend. He was not sure what the response would be if he attempted to gain access through these brutes blocking his way. After a few steps, he had to try. He tapped the closest one on his shoulder cautiously. The huge, rough man turned eyeing David with a warning. David couldn't help himself. He had to get closer to his friend. He motioned as respectfully as he could while remaining silent. The man let him pass, touching his fellow in front to let him know David was coming through. David was stunned at the response; but, soon decided it was respect for their leader, not for him, that had gained him any access to the lead position.

The young leader stopped as David approached. He held up his hand without turning to stop his men. He didn't look back, but he spoke quietly to David somehow knowing he was there behind him. "Look," he whispered pointing straight up. There at the top of the cliff he could see the pursuers lining the edge as they trudged along.

They stood there for a long time watching as the day grew darker and the shadows grew longer in the deep and quiet valley. Nothing was said. Everyone waited for a sign from their leader. Finally, without a word he continued on, still observing the top edge.

Within a few hundred paces, they came upon a flat grassy area surrounded by blue wildflowers and beds of yellow buttercups. The grass was long and lush. Off to the right, a deep, green pool of water rippled, surrounded by reeds and low hanging trees with flowering vines looping through the branches. Birds were singing.

The evening began to grow darker, causing the shapes of the men at the top to cast shadows like long and looming giants reaching into the valley. The men sat silently by the pool of water filling their containers and scooping mouthfuls as they knelt at its side. David drank a few handfuls and lied down on the thick, grassy bank.

The scent of honeysuckle and wild roses wafted under his nostrils as a breeze blew past. The combination of solitude and the peaceful, still green pool of water restored his soul even though the valley was looming with the impending threat of death proposed by the ever-lengthening shadows of the pursuers. David slept. They both slept.

The men were moving before morning broke. David's body was growing stronger. They circled the valley moving across to the side they had originally climbed and began ascending upward again. David smiled. He realized what this young man was up to. They continued up the deep cliff climbing all day and all night, not stopping to rest.

When morning broke again, they stopped, allowing the men to sit and rest and eat a few bites of nourishment from their pouches. The roughest and biggest of them was seated next to David, who was seated next to the leader. He offered David a morsel. This small act from so strong and rugged a fellow sent a wave of happiness through David's soul. Here was a gesture of the acceptance and respect he desired. The dry morsel of bread was more refreshing than any taco or burger he had ever eaten. He was being nourished beyond the physical. His very soul felt nourished.

The young leader also offered a piece of meat to David who, in turn, ripped off a corner and handed it to the man sitting next to him. He took it with a nod and ate heartily. David could see out of the corner of his eye that the young leader was smiling slightly and was himself eating heartily.

They sat there for over an hour. The food and the rising sun began to tire the men. David yawned, in unison with several of the men. David's friend stood and stretched, as did the rest. Pulling their belongings back around their waists and over their shoulders, they began to march along the edge again. David could see that as they walked they grew more stealthy, slowing their pace slightly to silence their steps as they went.

When night came upon them again, they continued on carefully in the light of the moon. Suddenly, the leader stopped, listening. David could hear the muffled distant sounds of voices. They continued, closing in on the sounds carefully.

David could hear the sounds were closer now, and below them. The leader took his arm, moved along silently, and then gently pulled him into a cave-like entrance on the side of the path. The men followed him inside carefully pulling off their packs. They walked to the edge of the cave's entrance and listened to the sounds below. Their pursuers were just beneath them. The big man next to David unconsciously placed his hand on the sword sheathed on his belt. A look of determination caused his eyes to squint and his jaws to set. The young leader laid his hand on the other fellow's hand, giving him a look that made the other shake his head with a combination of acceptance and disagreement, but he took his hand off his sword shaking his head again. He walked to the side of the cave and sat with his head resting back against the wall. His eyes were still on his leader, ready for instant action if called upon. David's friend stood at the entrance of the cave. David stood with him. They had not spoken for a long while.

"Come, David," he spoke quietly while motioning to the large man. The rest of the men stood and the leader motioned them to stay. Taking David and the large man with him, he exited the cave and began a quiet and quick descent toward the sound of the voices. David's heart was pounding in his ears. He was not afraid. He was excited that he was not. He felt exhilaration, expectation, and a strange joy at being a part of something beyond himself. He knew this was not his story; yet, he was experiencing it, allowed to be a part of something big! He belonged, even though he really didn't.

The voices grew closer. David could hear conversations. The three men squatted just outside the camp of their pursuers. They waited. Conversations were fading into the dark shadows of night, replaced by snores and the grunting of tired soldiers. The leader turned to his companions holding his hand up again warning them to stay and be still. Silently, he moved into the camp. David could not see his form in the darkness once he was a few feet away. The moon had been shadowed temporarily by dark night clouds, shutting off most of the light they had traveled by. His heart was thudding. He wanted to follow. He was anxious to know his friend was safe. He felt it was wrong to stay here hiding while his friend moved into the dangers of the sleeping camp of men.

He started to move and was stopped by the grasp of a huge hand, halting his body, the force of the grasp shooting pain through his wrist and arm. David stopped. He looked toward the big man holding him, barely able to make out his face. He was looking right at David. The hand released him and gave him a quick, friendly rub on his shoulder. David understood. He was to be still.

The minutes seemed like hours. Tears were threatening to spill. David longed to be at his friend's side. He had grown to admire and love this young man. He was strong and gentle. He was wise and witty. He was bold and cautious. He was a respected leader. Enormous, strong, rough men respected him. He sang gentle songs of love and deep emotions. It was easy to love him.

David knew this man beside him felt the same way. He had seen it on his face as David took the lead position. He had seen it on the other men's faces as he spoke to them. He commanded respect without a word of demanding it.

As silently as he had left, the leader was back in their company, patting David's back and moving past him. David followed with the other man at his back. His sword had been silently unsheathed.

The cloud slowly left the moon's face, lighting the way as they journeyed back up to the cave. The leader stepped inside, stopping at its entrance, sitting, and singing softly. David could not make out the words. He was singing something about shepherds, sheep, and deep, green pools.

David awakened with a start at a shout from the entrance of the cave. His leader was shouting to the camp below! David's heart felt like it would stop. He had dozed off to the sound of soft, beautiful singing. Now, he had been startled awake by a shout!

"What on earth is he doing exposing his place to those who pursue him?" David thought. He jumped up, stumbling over himself as he stood. The rest of the men were on their feet already. They were standing with swords ready.

David heard an answer from the camp below. The young leader stepped out of safety into the open and David's heart pounded in his ears again. He saw the young man hold up a spear in one hand and a sword in the other. Explaining in loud shouts to the camp below how he had invaded them the night before, David's friend was obviously talking to one particular person. He told him how he could have killed him in the night.

"See," he was shouting. "Look! I could have ended this pursuit myself, my friend. I was with you as you slept. Your life was mine to take."

David noticed a sound in his friend's voice. His words broke as if holding back a cry. "Why do you wish to end my life, when I wish you to live, my brother and my king?" Again, the voice broke as if he would break into weeping.

There was silence below, but only for a few seconds. Then, sorrowfully and repentantly, a voice shouted back apologies and begged forgiveness. The men in the cave looked at each other incredulously! The leaders of both camps called back and forth for a while.

David stepped forward to his friend's side, looking at the huge man to stop him. He didn't. David stood by his friend. Together, they watched the troop of soldiers break camp below and march away. Nothing was said between the two. Both Davids were silent as they watched. Once, the leader looked at David and then, quickly looked away. Turning, he walked into the cave and sat with his back to his men. David could hear him speaking. It was obvious he wanted solitude. David wanted to go to him, but didn't. Instead, he looked at the huge fellow and then at the rest of the men. All were watching their leader in silent regard.

David lied back on the ground with his head on his hands and let the pent up emotions of the night flow down his face and spill onto the ground. He wept from somewhere deep inside. He could feel his friend's pain right then. He was not weeping for himself this time. He wept with his friend. He wept as he drifted off into a light sleep. Again, his dreams carried him away.

He dreamed of distant lands. He saw people of all nationalities. All were weeping and sorrowful. David could feel their pain in the same way he had felt his friend's pain. This was sorrow beyond any he had known. He began to weep harder and harder and was crying in deep and loud cries. His stomach was tight and his body was heaving from the depth of his soul. He was crying with and for the nations of weeping people. He could feel their pain and sorrow. He cried as if their sorrows were his own. He cried as if his own soul was breaking.

"David!" The voice was not whispering. "David!" He felt someone shake him to awaken him.

"Wake, Friend!" David's eyes opened to his friend's smiling face. "Come! Eat!" The young man stared into David's eyes. They looked at each other for a brief second. David felt he could see into his soul. The other young man gave a single nod. David looked away, and then turned away. He rolled himself to a standing position, stretching his arms up. He twisted his back to one side, and then the other. He let out a long yawn and shook his arms as if to remove the nightmares of his heart. The men were talking, laughing, and sharing morsels of food. David looked at the food with wonder.

"From the camp below," the huge man explained in response to David's look of wonderment, "left in their rush to leave!" He let out a chuckle. The young leader looked up suddenly at this statement. David noticed the look. He was sure that the young leader did not think the food was left accidentally or in the rush of leaving. David did not think so either. Again, they glanced at each other knowingly.

David took a piece of bread and ate it heartily. He was hungry. He knew his experiences and his dreams had taken him to a new place. He had experienced a different sense of companionship and connection. He had become one with his friend in the spirit. This unity was more fulfilling than the food. He pondered over of the depth of weeping for his friend's sorrow. He thought of how he had actually felt it himself. His dreams had connected his spirit with the spirits of nations. He had felt their hurt and his soul had been poured out for them. Strangely, that too was a sorrowfully fulfilling place of connection. He felt a strange awareness of the belonging he had longed for. It was not what he had imagined it would be.

"Who would have thought that sorrow could be comforting," he thought out loud.

"Or that suffering could bring relief." The young leader answered.

"Or that by surrendering, you could escape." David shot back with a mouthful of bread.

The young leader nodded, with a smile. "Or that by serving, you could gain a servant." He spoke with mirth as he handed David another morsel.

David chuckled silently, smiling and chewing at the same time.

After eating, the men all slept again. David was not sure how long they slept. He had lost track of time. It was daylight again when they awakened. They left the cave traveling back to the cave behind the waterfall. They stepped into its shelter, once again getting wet as they passed through. They all bathed in the still water inside the cave. As he soaked in the water, he gazed at the sparkling walls again. The streaks of silver and gold glistened in the rays of light shining through the falling water.

He dunked his head under the water several times. When he climbed out, he shook as much of the water from his garment as he could. He walked over to the boulder he had used the first night and sat on it. The leader exited the water after a while and sat next to David on the ground. David immediately stood offering the leader the boulder, who accepted the gesture.

"Gained a servant," he said, smiling at David. David smiled back and sat next to him.

"Tell me about Him," The leader commanded. "Tell me about the Messiah."

"Shouldn't *you* be telling *me* about Him?" David asked. The young man's expression was deeply wistful and questioning. David felt the seriousness of this look.

"Well," David began. "I can't tell you as much as I should be able to. I did meet Him, at least once. Like I told you, I met Him when He took my place. I was the one who should have died that day. It was my cross, you see. He never sinned. I did."

"He died?"

"He was nailed on a cross after being beaten so badly you could barely see he had a face! At first, it was me. I mean, well, I woke up under that cross with sweat and vomit and pain that can't be described. I felt nauseated and feverish. My body ached and stung like it was on fire everywhere, even my face. I couldn't raise my head. It was pressed into the dirt and vomit was in my mouth. I couldn't get it out or breathe. I tried to lift my head. It was pounding so hard and something heavy was holding it down. Someone kicked me in the side. It felt like the kick knocked the rest of my breath out and I couldn't bring in any air. I felt myself going unconscious from the pain and the vomit I was choking on. I couldn't breathe!

Then suddenly, I could breathe. The weight was lifted. I looked and there was this man's beaten and swollen face, blood and dirt clinging to swollen eyes that were barely open. He said, 'I'll do it for you.'" David was weeping as he relived the memory. "He took my place and died for me. They killed Him instead of me!"

David saw a strange look on his friend's face, but he continued. He was killed and they buried Him in a cave. He came alive again after three days." David had to tell the story as he had remembered it, not from experience, but from what he had heard and read. "He took my place. I knew the story about it. I didn't know how it really was until I was there. He took my place!

Everything I did that was wrong in my life, He had done right. He showed me. He showed me myself. I was traveling through space seeing all these different things I had done in my life. He showed me Himself doing just the opposite. He showed me my ways of living life. Then, He showed me His in contrast. I was the one who should have died that day! I knew it! I knew it more than I ever have known it. They killed Him instead of me. He never did any of the stuff I did. He didn't do anything wrong at all. He showed me that first. I did. I did everything wrong. It should have been me. It was awful!" David was crying freely. "It hurt so bad! It was so scary. I was so afraid! I couldn't breathe and my head was…" David couldn't go on.

"Who would have thought that suffering could bring relief? Who would have thought that by serving, you could gain a servant? Who would have thought that by dying you could bring life?" The young leader stood and walked away as he was speaking.

Chapter 12

David sat for a long time. He had left his home wanting to find God. He had always wanted to know the feeling of belonging and acceptance. He had spent years trying to find companionship and relationship. He had found this by serving someone else. He had discovered relationship by connecting with someone else's sorrow. He had wanted to experience life and not be afraid. He had learned how by facing sure death. He had found what he was searching for in the most unusual of circumstances.

He had given up trying to control his destiny and had witnessed the most bizarre and wonderful of destinations. He had become aware of his worthless existence, and then discovered his real worth when someone who had worth died so he wouldn't have to.

He had found that there is no way to run away from the biggest distraction to recognizing or discovering God, himself and his own desires. He had become lost in some strange hand of fate and had found himself in the process. Most of all, he had found God was always very near in everything.

He knew now how precious his life was. He had discovered recognition and worth, and yes, even fame and value. He was valuable, important, and remembered by God. He was important and thought of by the most important being ever. He was never forgotten, not for even a second. He was loved beyond any measure he could have hoped for. He was connected with God by God's very own thoughts. That connection gave him access to everything he could dream of, desire, or hope for. He already had it all, every desire and dream. Nothing he could do could ever give him more. He had it all already. No failure or lack on his part could get in his way. He didn't have to be good or strong or wealthy. He was David, God's very own friend, with everything at his command, should he choose it. He was because God is, and because God wanted him. He had been chosen to be by God Himself! He had discovered who he really was by discovering who he was not.

David closed his eyes and raised his hands in surrender. He could hear the sound of his friend's voice in the cave. He could hear the sound, "I am…." in the falling of the water as his friend's voice rose in harmony. He heard the sound of wings beating in the air. He felt himself rising and spiraling. He kept his eyes closed, waiting. What he was waiting for he wasn't sure. He was ready for whatever his next adventure might be.

The sounds grew louder and deafening. The water was beating against the rocks. "I am…" The voice of his friend rose in beautiful and thrilling notes. The sound of the wings grew louder and louder. Trumpets blew in the distance. He felt himself losing all sense of consciousness. He felt peaceful, content, fulfilled, alive, and unafraid.

David leaned his head back with an expectant smile, ready. He took a deep breath as he fell into unconsciousness. "Whatever it is," he thought, "I will not be afraid. I will experience it to its fullest. I will trust Him. I will learn. I will grow. I will become like Him. I will….."

David rubbed his eyes with his sleeve as he awakened. His whole body felt stiff. He yawned and started to turn to his side. His entire body went tense as he sat up, realizing he was waking up on the dusty lane across from the dry field.

"What…?" He looked around as disappointment engulfed him. He felt his shoulders aching and shooting pains hurt his neck. His hips felt bruised. He stood up slowly, his back so sore he could barely stand straight. He stared across at the empty field. He rubbed his tired eyes with his sleeve again. As his eyes started to burn, he realized his sleeve was covered with the dust from the lane. He smelled his arm. It smelled dusty and musky. He looked down at his clothes and saw that they were stiff with sweat and dust.

David was confused. He looked around with deep disappointment. He picked up his belongings, shaking off the dust. He wasn't able to think clearly. He walked slowly across the lane and out into the field. Nothing was there. He walked to where he had first found the vehicle. The grass was dry and long in the spot where the vehicle had been. He leaned down to feel it. It hurt to bend. David felt a mixture of disappointment, confusion, and pain. He slowly stood and stretched his back, turning to one side and then the other, listening to the crackle of his spine adjusting. With drooping shoulders, he began to walk to the lane, and then down the road to where he had found the waterfall before.

He sat beside the pool listening to the water. Finally, he stepped in and soaked for several minutes. He swam until he felt a little less stiff and dirty. Then, he sat on the bank listening to the water, pondering what had happened to him. He wondered if he had been dreaming this whole time. So much had happened! If this had been a dream, he must have been sleeping a lifetime!

The sound of the water reminded him of the voice. He tried to hear the sound of "I am…." coming from the water. It took a long time and concentration, but after a while, he began to think he could hear it vaguely. He was hungry and his stomach felt sick. He looked around to see if anyone was near, remembering the farmer. Out loud, he spoke, "I wonder where he is."

"I am ….here," David thought at first the sound had come from the water. Then, turning he saw the farmer walking up with a basket of food.

"Hey," said David, "I was just thinking about you." David's voice was flat.

"You hungry, Friend?"

David felt no hesitation in admitting he was hungry. Too much had happened! Dream or not, David had lived several lifetimes and felt no need for pride. In fact, he was not sure if at that moment he could care about anything. He had not forgotten his exhilaration only moments before. He remembered. But, he could not feel it now. He felt lost in a fog of loss and depression. Here he was, all alone with himself again.

He took the basket and devoured everything in it before he realized it might not have all been for him. With his mouth still full of the last bite, he looked up in apology at the farmer.

The farmer smiled. "Son, it's time for you to go home."

"I need to get going is what I need to do," David answered the farmer. "I am supposed to be on a journey." His voice was filled with sarcasm and discouragement. "I have spent my entire life dreaming!"

David was holding nothing back. "I have always dreamed about being rich. I've dreamed about building cars and inventing engines and…. all I ever do is dream! I am a dreamer! I am nothing but a dreamer!" David was filled with disappointment in himself. Tears stung at his eyes.

"Why couldn't this have been real?" He had turned and was shouting at the waterfall. "Why? I thought I had found you!" Tears were streaming down David's disappointed face. David was aware he had used the word "I" several times. The thought about being his own biggest distraction to recognizing God in his life was there for only a brief second.

David stared at the waterfall listening to the sound. "I am…I am…" He began to hear something else. He strained with all his might to make out the words. "I am the same…." David held his breath to hear, "I am the same yesterday, today, and forever." He let his breath out slowly, listening even closer. All other sounds faded except the water, "I am...I am the sound of living water. I am the first and the last. I am the one who will be, the one who was, and the one who is."

"God always is." It was the farmer. David looked at him. "God always is, He always was, and He always will be. He is not limited by time or space or even by what you define as reality or existence. He just *is* and you get to be in on it."

"Son, it is time to go home now," repeated the farmer gently. He reached down to help David up. “Walk and talk with me a moment,” he spoke to David with utter kindness in his voice.

David felt himself lean against the farmer when he wrapped his arm around David’s shoulder walking beside him. David’s thoughts were surging through his tired and disappointed mind. He did not want to go back to searching for himself. He did not want to be his old self again! He wanted to hold onto all he had experienced in his dreams. He wanted to be different like his friend David. He wanted to remember how to find God and not to be searching for life instead of living it. He had changed in his dreams. He had become someone else and did not want to return to his old way of viewing life or God!

“You are a great young man, David. God called you to find Him and look for Him with your whole heart. You have done that.”

“How? Sleeping? Dreaming?” David’s voice was still sarcastic and filled with sorrow and disappointment.

The farmer chuckled. “Nope, before you took your first step on this journey. And everyplace you’ve been on it. And… at the water a few minutes ago.”

“What?” David stopped and looked at the farmer.

The farmer's eyes seemed to be blazing and on fire as the sun glinted off the amber irises. Looking deeply into David's eyes, he repeated. "At the water a few minutes ago when you tried to hear the voice in the water. You have to search in everything to find Him. He is in everything. He is here. He is in the sound of the water and the breath of the air you breathe.

Don't be distracted by your own life, by situations, sorrows, fears, or suffering. Those things have to be for now. Just look for Him and find Him in whatever and wherever you find yourself. He is not far away. He exists in the suffering. He exists in the relief. He exists in the loss. He exists in the gain. Yes, He exists in the very creation around you. He is not hard to find. He is right there.

What makes it seem hard is getting past the distraction of your own existence. When that is out of the way, you see He is right there all the time. You find Him when you search for Him with all your heart, beyond yourself and your own desires. Not because He is distant, but because your heart gets in the way when it is not His totally. He exists for you when and where you let Him in your life."

David was silent. He tried to take in what the farmer meant.

"He exists when you allow Him to live through you. David, He gave up the chance to exist here in this world with you. He was here, in person. He was here in the Garden. He was here as a baby, as a youth, as a man. He could have lived a life right here where you could easily see Him. He could have lived experiencing the fullness of companionship, relationship, belonging, acceptance, and love. The very things you search for. He could have chosen that.

He found you crushed under the weight of sin and death, unable to breathe life, bruised, and beaten. He took your place! He took it so you could live. He took *your* death for you." He stopped for a minute to let David feel what he was saying. "He took you there, so you could see. It was an exchange though, that moment."

David looked at the farmer, waiting. "It was an exchange. He took your place, giving up His chance to live and experience all of those things you wish for. He gave them up for you.

Now, it's His turn to live. You must let Him experience those things through you. It's your turn to die…to yourself, and let Him live, so that it is no longer you who lives, but He who lives in you. It's His turn. You have to learn to live and love your life, every single part of it, including the pain and sorrow, as well as the joy and gladness.

All of it should be embraced and experienced to the fullest, allowing Him to live and love through you. He is right there. Let your heart become His heart, and then… well, it won't be hard to search for Him with all of it. He will be right there in every experience of life, good and bad."

"It is time to go home now and discover God where you are at every moment. He is everywhere you are and in everything around you.

You have been on a journey with Him since you became His thought, before you were born, at the beginning. You will be on His mind now and always. You exist because of Him. You exist for Him.

He desires to walk and talk with you and take you places you have never even dreamed of. He is always with you. Even if you should go to the ends of the earth, to the highest heights on the wings of the wind, or to the depths of the deepest sea, He is there with you. All you have to do is open your eyes, open your ears, and open your heart. There, you will recognize and feel Him. Go home, Son."

David sighed. His shoulders were drooping. He was trying to take in what the farmer was saying. Truly, he was.

"But, well, was I dreaming? Was any of this real? What about…?" Before he could ask it, the farmer looked into David's eyes. The farmer's amber eyes were on fire. The flame from them was searing through him.

"Son, your whole existence is an experience with God. He is not limited by time, by dreams, by your explanation of things. You need to stop seeking for explanations. Explanations just lead to more questions. You never need an explanation to experience. You need an experience to experience. Go and experience who I am…" The farmer smiled and looked down pulling up his sleeves and removing his gloves. He reached out to shake David's hand.

"Time to go home, Son," the farmer repeated. As David reached to grasp his hand, he noticed the scars. David looked up with wonder, staring into the farmer's blazing eyes. He could feel the fire of intense love warming his heart.

"It's true then." David started to speak. As he did, the farmer's face began to fade. David looked at the hand grasping his as it also faded, leaving his hand held out in midair. The faint scent of roses began to fill the air, increasing, until once again, he could smell roses, candles, and bread. He closed his eyes and dropped his hand, breathing deeply. He felt a waft of wind and looked down to see his shirt moving with the breeze.

David smiled. He nodded. Yes, he was ready for the next big adventure! Turning to pick up his belongings, he patted the pencil in his pocket. He swung his backpack up on his back and took one last look at the empty field. The wind sent a sudden strong breeze causing the grass to lie flat and the trees down the lane to bow. He nodded again as a goodbye. The air grew still and he turned to begin his trek home.

The sun was warm on his back. Birds were singing in the distance. As he walked, he could hear the distant sound of a hollow, flute-like instrument. The music warmed his heart and one lone tear trickled down his cheek, stopping briefly at the corner of his smile.

NOT THE END

Made in the USA
Columbia, SC
26 September 2023